The Sky is Changing

The Sky is Changing

Zoë Jenny

Legend Press
Independent Book Publisher

Legend Press Ltd, 2 London Wall Buildings,
London EC2M 5UU
info@legend-paperbooks.co.uk
www.legendpress.co.uk

Contents © Zoë Jenny 2010

British Library Cataloguing in Publication Data available.

ISBN 978-1-9065581-7-8

Set in Times
Prin~~ted by LE Print Ltd, Snackford, Somerset~~

Legend Press
Independent Book Publisher

Selected other works by
Zoë Jenny

The Pollen Room
The Call of The Conch Shell
A Fast Life
The Portrait

The Pollen Room is the all-time best-selling debut novel by a Swiss author and has been translated into 27 languages. This is Zoë Jenny's first novel written in English.

Praise for Zoë Jenny

'In her apartment in Basel's old town, however, wearing earplugs to block out the noise of the trams and with sheaves of writing paper at her side, she achieved something momentous: writing by hand, she composed a 134-page novel that has become the talk of Swiss literary circles.' *NEW YORK TIMES*

'As Jo's child's eye narration covers everything from a haircut to an abortion in the same mesmeric deadpan style, it soon becomes apparent that this is not so much a narrative as a portrait of a state of mind in extremis... At times reminiscent of both Plath and Hemingway – a memorable debut.' *SUNDAY TIMES*

'Zoë Jenny's account of a marriage break-up is both barmy and believable and her words are an exciting mish-mash of dreamy images and reminding realism.' *THE TIMES*

'The story of a psyche, but one unadorned by self-conscious or analytical comment, mediated through poetic detail and precise, concrete images. The prose is spare, assured and evocative, the tone matter-of-fact and utterly without self-pity... There's an undertow of danger lurking beneath the surface which makes you want to re-read this intriguing, haunting novel as soon as you've finished it.' *OBSERVER*

'A moving account of a disturbed childhood, and the prose works many of its best effects through under-statement and absences.' *SUNDAY TELEGRAPH*

About the author

Zoë Jenny's first novel *The Pollen Room* was the all-time bestselling debut by a Swiss author. Translated into 27 languages, it has won huge critical acclaim worldwide. Her published novels since include, *The Call of the Conch Shell*, *A Fast Life* and *The Portrait* and Zoë Jenny is widely regarded as one of the best writers of her generation.

With *The Sky is Changing* her first novel to be written in English, she has become one of the first writers to create original fiction in more than one language.

Zoë Jenny was born in Basel, Switzerland, in 1974. After years of travelling and living in New York and Berlin, she has now settled in London.

For Matthew

*

The rosebush was already there when they moved in. Someone must have planted it many years ago; perhaps it had only been a little plant back then and the person who put it in the earth never had the chance to see it in full bloom. Intertwined with the passion-flower, the roses had climbed up and covered almost half of the brick wall at the back of the garden. The scarlet and purple flowers were so vibrant, it surprised Claire that something so beautiful was able to grow in this little dark backyard, and she couldn't help but hesitate before she snipped off a bunch of roses with the secateurs. There was something sacrilegous about it, like when she had taken that glorious orchid while on a walk, which had then wilted by the time they got home. Why did she have to take it; wasn't it enough just to look at it? But this time, the flowers weren't for herself.

Claire looked up into the bright blue sky and followed the white jetstream of a plane leaving London. How quickly this year had passed, she thought. How good the world was at looking normal and concealing its tragedies.

"Let's go," Anthony shouted from inside the kitchen. "I haven't got all day!"

Claire smiled as she knew that while it sounded as if he had something very important to do, he just wanted to be back in time for the match.

"You don't have to come, you know. I can go by myself," she said.

He didn't even answer, just rushing out of the house instead.

It was a hot, humid day. City Road was jammed with traffic and a line of buses moved sluggishly forward, like a herd of ancient animals slowly dying in the sun.

"Don't you want to try again?" Anthony asked tentatively when they reached Upper Street, Angel Tube station just a few steps away. "It's only one single stop to King's Cross, you know."

Claire shook her head.

"You don't want me to have a heart attack, do you?"

It happened shortly after the bombings a year ago, somewhere on the Northern Line. It was rush hour, and Claire had found herself pushed to the back of the carriage, unable to move. People were swaying with every turn, and she could feel the cumulative weight of the passengers smothering her. Her heart was racing in her chest so hard it was as if a living creature was trying to get out. 'Calm down, for God's sake,' she had said to herself, but her heart just went faster. The noise of creaking metal and rattling wheels cutting through the darkness at high speed gave her a drowning sensation. Staring at the door and counting the seconds, she remembered the expression: 'soft target'. She could die here with all these strangers, in an instant, just like that. The fear and aggression in the air was almost palpable; everyone on survival. Suddenly something inside her changed, a sudden diffusion of chemicals in her brain. She had to get out of there, right then.

With both her elbows she pushed people aside. Someone swore at her, "Stupid bitch", but she didn't care, she was someone else now, brutish, raw, animal-like. She would have punched anyone who dared to stand in her way. These weren't people anymore, just obstacles, stinking, hateful flesh.

When Claire had finally emerged from the Tube, stepping into the daylight, she was covered in sweat and out of breath, her mouth dry. Stumbling into the toi-let of a nearby Starbucks, she looked at her face in the mirror: it wasn't just pale, it was as white as a sheet. Her knees weak and shaky, completely exhausted, she sat on the lid of the toilet seat to recover. She propped her head in her hands, ashamed of herself; she couldn't believe that she had behaved like that. For a brief moment she had actually lost her mind.

After that incident Claire had decided to never, ever

go down there again and was relieved that Anthony didn't insist on using the Tube. Even though he was convinced it was just one of her fads that would be forgotten with time, he had bought her a scooter as a gift.

Pentonville Road was a long stretch, and Claire carried the flowers head down so they wouldn't wilt as quickly in the heat. Anthony checked his BlackBerry and there was a Happy Birthday greeting from his mother. He read it somewhat disappointed, as if he had expected it to be from someone else. Claire felt sorry for him, that they had to do this on his birthday – that this day was a day of grief for so many.

She could see other people with flowers now, someone even carrying a giant teddy bear under his arm. A large crowd had gathered just a few metres to the right of King's Cross station entrance. There was a little square behind some railings with a tree in the middle, at night a seedy place where drug dealers and prostitutes hang out.

Now there were dozens of people creating a temporary memorial, and Anthony and Claire joined the queue, waiting for their turn. A security guard made sure that not everyone went in at once. Policemen were protecting the site, batons and guns at the ready. Most people just laid down their flowers and left, but some were kneeling in front of a photograph or wreath, praying.

Even though King's Cross was a busy, noisy spot, on this particular day there was a strange silence, interrupted only by announcements from the loudspeakers inside the station. Claire was looking at the photographs and children's drawings. There were flowers everywhere, some still wrapped in foil, sweating away in the sun, releasing their sweet, heavy scent. The smell of death, Claire thought, and she laid the roses next to a photograph mounted on a piece of cardboard. It showed a young girl with short blond hair. Underneath, in big red letters, was written 'Why?'

A man next to her wept, holding on to the picture of a woman, almost tearing it apart. Suddenly he let go of it and left, looking around with darting eyes. He appeared completely lost, as if in panic, not knowing where to go. Eventually he disappeared into the shadowy hall of the station.

They didn't talk on their way back. One of the reasons she loved him so much was that Anthony always seemed to know when it was time to be silent. She touched his hand with her finger, briefly and gently, as if to reassure herself it was real, that if needed there was this hand she could grab and hold on to.

The noise of the football on the telly filled the afternoon. It was a welcome distraction and had the comforting sound of normality, the rhythm of everyday life.

Claire was in her room upstairs, sitting at the desk by the window surfing the internet. There were speeches and readings in Regent's Park and several other commemorative events all over London. She found a website with photos and a short biography for each of the 52 victims. There it was again, the picture of the blond girl. She was from Poland, 27-years-old, and had been on her way to work that morning – perhaps thinking of her next trip back home to her family in Krakow when the bomb hit. They identified her because they found a fragment of her tooth in the rubble.

Claire wondered how her parents had learnt of her death. They couldn't get her corpse back in a coffin. There was no corpse. There weren't even ashes. Maybe one morning her parents had received a package, bearing a London postmark, containing that fragment of their daughter's tooth.

Claire scrolled up and down the photographs. All these faces were still fresh in the memory of the public, but they would be soon forgotten. A year after the bombings she had brought flowers, but would they do it the following year and the year after that? She doubted it.

Claire realised that people die twice and it's the second death that's final – when no one remembers you anymore, when all that remains of your existence is wiped out, then you are completely and truly gone.

She turned off the computer. From downstairs she could hear Anthony shouting and clapping his hands in excitment. Arsenal were winning. He would be in a good mood tonight and they were going out to celebrate his 33rd birthday.

Looking out of the window, Claire could see the evening sun about to disappear behind the rooftops and chimneys of Islington, the sky red and orange, slowly turning darker.

Anthony was usually reluctant to do anything on his birthday, but when she told him they were going out for dinner with some friends he seemed flattered that she had made the effort.

He liked the Moroccan restaurant, with its low, round tables and dark little corners where people could play boardgames and drink sweet mint tea served in tiny glasses.

Sam, Christine and David were already there when they arrived, sharing a big mezze platter. Sam and Christine had just come back from India and their photos circulated around the table. Pictures of women in colourful saris on a backdrop of lush green, children on a roadside, waving, Christine on her bike, wearing a weather-beaten helmet. It had always been one of Sam's dreams, riding around India on a motorbike, and Christine had got her licence just for the holiday.

Claire was impressed by Christine's courage, and the fact that she was 37, childless and completely relaxed about it. One night she had asked her whether she was anxious to get pregnant. "We love to travel, and if it happens that's great, but, if it doesn't, I'm not going to beat myself up about it."

Claire felt instantly relieved and comfortable in her company. Both Christine and Sam were teachers, and their double income and generous holidays allowed them to travel. They always seemed to have just come back from some faraway place: Easter Island, Galapagos, Vietnam. There was a constant whiff of adventure and foreign lands about them.

Sitting next to her, Claire was admiring an intricate silver bracelet on Christine's tanned wrist that she had bought for next to nothing in a market somewhere in Rajasthan.

"It would be impossible for you to leave Britain," said Sam in a loud voice to David. "You would die of hunger."

David, one of Anthony's work colleagues, notoriously neurotic when it came to food, was raving about a place in Notting Hill where one could get wheat grass shoots.

"Probably one of the reasons why you are still single," said Anthony, "is your grassy breath."

They had tried to hook David up several times, but to no avail. Especially with Sadie, which had been the biggest disaster so far. "How could you send me a vegetarian?" she had said after she'd invited David to one of her dinner parties. Sadie was an excellent and keen cook, and told them how David had picked out the vegetables from her slow-cooked beef casserole.

For Sadie this was not only a turn off, but a complete insult. "A man who doesn't eat meat must be rubbish in bed," she once concluded.

"My body is my temple," David had replied in his defence when they asked how the evening with Sadie had gone. "She even eats dead animals for breakfast!"

Anthony and Claire were laughing as he told them. "That's what it comes down to," Anthony commented, "food. Even falling in love is dietary related. Sadie is a bloody carnivore and David's a cow. I can't believe we even let them near each other."

They had just finished their first course when Sadie arrived with her new boyfriend, Paolo, in tow, whom she introduced proudly. He was from Brazil, and Claire knew immediately that he must have something to do with dancing; she could tell from his upright posture and precise, slow movements and there was a pride in the way he carried himself that only dancers have.

'Shame it's not going to last long,' Claire thought, offering him a chair. Sadie never had a boyfriend for very long. Sometimes she had girlfriends, too, and they tended to stay a bit longer. One girl, ten years her junior, had even moved in with her, and at the time Sadie had become obsessed with the topic of same-sex marriage. When the girl left her for an artist, Sadie claimed her "heart had been broken", and from then on she changed her boyfriends in quick succession.

Sadie was 42 but young at heart. She exuded in abundance what Anthony called "*joie de vivre*". When she entered a room the chemical composition of the air seemed to change. Everyone looked at her, men and woman alike. The one thing that struck Claire most about Sadie was the fact that her mature beauty seemed far more powerful and threatening than the obvious beauty of youth could ever be.

David hugged her, tapping her shoulder in a manner old friends do. He was probably just relieved he didn't have to put up with her himself; everything about Sadie was much too much for him. Claire almost laughed out loud – seeing them together, she realised it was the most unlikely match.

Paolo and David got immediately engrossed in a conversation about some new action film. Claire wondered whether Paolo knew that Sadie was bisexual, and whether that played a part in his being attracted to her. Maybe it was something shifty in his eyes, or his apparent confidence that made Claire uncomfortable about him. He was probably just too good looking – in an obvious sort of way. She had always been suspicious if a man was too good-looking, especially when he knew it.

Anthony was sitting on the other side of the table. He was wearing the blue Paul Smith shirt she had given him for his birthday and his eyes and hair appeared darker, nearly black. Depending on the light, there was a hint of red in his hair – the Irish influence, a sign of his Celtic ancestry. His olive skin was unusually dark for a Brit and luckily he didn't share the pasty complexion of his family members. While they got burnt by the first hint of summer sun, he developed a tan almost immediately. His slender wrists and long hands implied sensitivity, and she liked the way his wristbones protruded under the skin when he gesticulated with his hands. She had always assumed he would be good at playing the piano. At times Claire wondered whether Anthony wasn't wasting creative capacity and whether it did his talents justice working as a junior analyst at HowlandRoberts. He was responsible for the pharmaceutical sector of this well-respected City firm, and his prospects there matched his ambition to climb the career ladder.

Anthony was explaining something to Sadie, elaboratly gesticulating. He liked to use them to great effect while talking, just like an Italian, she thought; it was entertaining to watch.

Sadie was laughing and nodding at what he said but, when he realised Claire was observing them, he winked at her – a quick, sexy gesture across the table, throwing it at her like a ball she was supposed to catch. She appreciated that he showed his attraction to her so openly, especially in front of Sadie.

Even though she regarded Sadie as one of her closest friends and trusted her a great deal, Sadie's sexiness, her sheer lust for life, meant that she was a natural enemy to the very convention of marriage. Sadie had in fact called herself unsuited to any sort of marital agreement. "I am married to life," she had said. "People need concepts like marriage to weather the storm of life, only to get shattered and disillusioned. Life doesn't follow rules and contracts; it never does."

However, Claire didn't think of her as a cynic, which made it even more difficult to dismiss her opinion. She had much too much warmth for that. Claire was the first to defend Sadie, but nevertheless harboured the faintest suspicion – and she hated herself for the thought and tried to reject it as paranoia – that Sadie was the kind of woman who had the ability to destroy an otherwise happy couple.

Sometimes Claire wondered what it was exactly that attracted her to Anthony. After all, he spent his days in an environment completely alien to her – in a world of numbers and projections. He seemed to follow a clear path and as a result was much more grounded than her. Until she had met him she was just floating around, rootless like a particle in a vast ocean forever moving, carried only by the unpredictibale current of life. Perhaps it was just the right timing and she was finally ready and willing to let someone take her on his way.

After all those years of wandering around, being with Anthony felt like resting on a island and for the first time she as able to take a deep breath.

Anthony broke her thoughts by waving at the waiter to order more wine.

"I'd much rather have a house in Tuscany; I could never live in France," Christine said.

"As it stands, we are not buying a house anywhere," Sam replied. "We just came back from a huge holiday..."

"I told her all I want is a little farm and a vineyard in California." David was talking about the girl from Santa Barbara again.

He showed photos of her on his BlackBerry. Claire had seen the pictures before. David had met this girl two years ago on a trip to California and was still talking about it like it was yesterday.

Mandy was vegetarian of course, clean and pretty. His dream woman.

"But you haven't seen her for ages. It's a fantasy. She's probably married by now and has a kid."

"We are e-mailing," David said defensively. Claire realised that the girl wasn't a fantasy for him. He lived with her, even if only in his mind.

"We talked on Skype recently," he added, looking down as if he had been whipped.

When Claire went to the toilet an hour later she could see the lipstick had crumbled in the corners of her mouth, her tongue blue from the red wine. While she was wiping her lips with a wet tissue she realised that for the last few hours she had actually forgotten what day it was. No one had mentioned that it was a year after the attacks, though maybe they just didn't want to spoil Anthony's birthday.

Coming back from the toilet, she looked at them from a distance. There they were, a bunch of joyous people, celebrating a birthday on a summer evening. And why shouldn't they? The scene was so innocent and happy, and it was good to see Anthony enjoying himself. When she returned to the table they were laughing hard about something; apparently she had just missed the punchline of a joke. The waiter then appeared with a ramshackle chocolate cake, a burning candle in it.

As they sang Happy Birthday, Sadie stood up, moving her hands as if conducting an orchestra. Paolo got up, put a hand around her waist and, to a song on the radio with a catchy samba rhythm, did a few moves. A true performer, Claire thought, instinctively rubbing her knee. She knew how it felt to be the centre of attention, presenting a perfectly trained body. She could tell immediately Paolo was a natural – he had the enviable ease of the South American, the rhythm ingrained in his bones. She knew he would ask her when he sat down and, putting his hand over her shoulder in a manly protective way, he turned to her.

"Sadie told me you are a dancer too?"

"Oh gosh no, not anymore anyway," Claire pointed quickly at her left knee. "I had a very bad cruciate ligament injury. It happened ages ago, but the meniscus is ruined. I'm teaching swimming lessons to children now."

She saw that he was pitying her, thinking of how many years of training she must have gone through, and so she added: "We are hoping to have children soon, so maybe it's better anyway. I couldn't possibly have a dance career now."

She heard her own words sound unconvincing, but Paolo nodded sympathetically. "Of course not, of course not," and after a pause, "It's so difficult to sustain a living."

He went on tell her about his DVD, a self-teaching course, which was selling well. She could understand why Sadie liked him. Apart from his looks, he had obviously come a long way. She was sure he had broken many hearts over the years, and Claire imagined all of the girls lined up who had waited for him after class, young and pretty. Easy prey. Against them, Sadie was a solid rock.

"A good catch," Anthony said later, referring to Paolo as they walked back home.

"He seems a nice guy," Claire agreed. "We should invite them over for dinner soon."

"You mean before they break up in a few weeks'

time." Anthony laughed.

Claire's hand was nestled in the back of his trouser pocket; she could feel the muscle of his buttocks moving. Their steps on the empty street made a hollow sound. It was a warm night, the moon cut perfectly in half.

"Soon the moon will be full again," Anthony said. There was something deeply comforting about a moon that was going to be full, Claire thought. It meant there was a rhythm and interplay they could do nothing about; it was just there, eternally, a bigger cycle that was following its own set of rules.

She felt tipsy when she got up the stairs to the bedroom. Naked, she sank into the white sheets, her body warm and saturated. She thought of her body as an egg; something very fragile that was now protected.

"Thank you," Anthony whispered into her ear, his hand running down her spine.

Lying back to back, their feet locked, she closed her eyes, already half-asleep.

She couldn't remember whether it was the light or the flapping that made her wake up only an hour later. A helicopter was hovering almost directly over their house.

"What's that?" Claire said, rubbing her eyes.

"They must be looking for someone," Anthony answered in a slumberous voice. "Just go back to sleep."

The helicopter flew north but came back only a minute later. It seemed to be flying in circles over Islington. She got up and looked behind the curtain down on to the street. She saw her scooter parked on the other side. The houses opposite, the cars, everything was immersed in the dim light of the streetlamp, unreal like an old black and white photograph. Only the flapping of the helicopter violently disturbed the placid scene, tearing it apart. It was Anthony's voice that finally released her from standing there, staring at the empty street, just as she realised it was fear, cold nameless fear, that was stirring in her chest.

*

Miss Zelda's voice came from the far corner of the room.

"Imagine your body is transparent," she said.

Claire didn't know how long she had been lying on the bed. They were alone; it was dark. She saw her own body gradually sink deeper and deeper, her limbs weightless, floating in a timeless space. The pain in her head had gone. She imagined in her brain a mass of blood vessels, painfully pulsating, the place of fears and nightmares. Now her head felt light and clear, like a room full of clutter that in one fell swoop had suddenly been tidied up. She opened her eyes, surprised to see the woman standing right next to her. She looked at her moonshaped face, a red-lipped smile hovering over her.

"Very good Claire. Well done," Miss Zelda said, taking her pulse. "Take your time."

However, Claire sat up immediately. She was wide awake and she realised exactly where she was. A wooden replica of a Buddha figure was sitting on a small desk. Miss Zelda put out the scented candle with two fingers before she switched on the light.

Claire jumped off the bed and slipped into her flip-flops. The walls were covered with pictures of babies. Babies in cots, babies wrapped in pink and baby blue blankets, lying in the arms of their smiling mothers. There must have been at least a hundred pictures. She wondered whether all these woman were former patients who had been lying on that very bed, being hypnotised just like she was. When she had started she had found the photos of all the happy mothers intimidating, but now she just looked into familiar faces as if they were cheering her on, encouraging her not to give up just yet.

Walking down Harley Street, Claire felt taller, as if the voice of the therapist had straightened her spine. The sun appeared from behind a cloud for just a few moments before it disappeared again. Claire imagined being someone else, someone with no purpose and no goal, walking down a street in a big city with no name, enjoying the warmness of the sun on her face. Suddenly, a strange freedom embraced her, a state of complete oblivion and the notion that happiness was nothing more than to forget oneself. Maybe Anthony was right and and the relaxation would help; maybe somehow, in some magical way, it would put things in place and make them work properly.

Claire went to Pauls in Marylebone High Street. She had a one-and-a-half hour gap before the next swimming lesson. It had become a ritual to go to Pauls after the hypnosis session. As soon as she sat down and ordered her Earl Grey tea with milk, two women with prams came in. One had a double buggy, cleverly designed with one seat stacked over another. She had twins, who were sleeping. When the women were seated, the second mother lifted her top and began to breastfeed her baby. Her naked, melon-sized breast hung out, blunt and white. She made no attempt to cover her breast – it was just there in the room for everyone to see.

Claire stirred her tea. It was difficult not to look. It had always made her slightly uncomfortable seeing women breastfeeding in public spaces; it was like passionately kissing couples, or men peeing on park trees. Why had some people the urge to exhibit intimate acts for everyone to see? For some time now she had noticed that wherever she went, in restaurants, cafes or shops, there would soon appear a horde of mothers with their brood, rubbing her nose in what she didn't have. This time, though, she wasn't all that envious. The baby puked, straight into the gap between its mothers breasts as if into a sick bag.

However, unperturbed, the mother just said, "In and out," as she wiped her breasts with a tissue. "It just goes in and comes back out again."

Claire wondered how old they were. Trying to guess their age was something she did almost automatically now when she saw mothers with their babies. To her relief they both looked older then her, probably in their early forties. She suspected that the twins were not conceived naturally. It had become a normal sight, women in their forties with twins and triplets, roaming the streets of London. They were raising the first generation of IVF children. Maybe she would have to become one of them. But Miss Zelda had told her, "Try everything else before you go down *that* route."

It had sounded as if it were the most desperate thing a couple could do, something that could stigmatise and even traumatise them forever. "I don't think you will need to do such an invasive treatment just yet," she had said, tapping her shoulder like a well-meaning friend, "you are still young." These comforting words enveloped her like a warming blanket. It was always a great relief to listen to Miss Zelda, and maybe it was true. Her body was still toned from the years of ballet training. In the gym she could easily outperform most twenty-year-olds, something she was quietly proud of. She was aware of the way she walked, in a upright posture with that gracious sway in her hips and the feet at a slight outward angle that revealed the dancer in her.

When she had married Anthony two years ago she had expected to get pregnant within six months. After all, that was what happened to the average, normal couple and there was nothing that had suggested they were anything other than that: normal.

After a year had passed, they went to a fertility clinic and all the tests turned out to be fine. "There is absolutely nothing wrong with you," the doctor had said. "There are no detectable medical reasons why you couldn't have a baby." They went home in a state of confusion.

At first she was just mildly disappointed when she saw the spots of blood in her knickers, but with the period recurring month after month she couldn't hide her frustration. It felt like a punishment, only she didn't know what for.

"You are only 33. We have plenty of time," Anthony said, trying to calm her down when she came out the bathroom, cursing and close to tears. But in the last few months Claire had sensed his growing disappointment. When they made love, his grasp was now impatient. Once she caught a glimpse of his face in the bathroom mirror. His expression was wild, almost angry.

The pillow talk, usually filled with laughter, had also slowly changed. When they lay in bed, staring at the ceiling, the tone of their voices got gradually lower as if they were ducking into the darkness of the night. They went over it again and again and, more often than not, their conversation ended in a row.

"But why doesn't it work if there isn't anything wrong?" she asked. "Maybe they missed something."

And then he said it. "It's all in your head, Claire."

She detected the hint of accusation in his voice. "What do you mean? Is it all my fault?" she said, looking at him.

"I didn't say that."

"You did." Her voice was trembling.

"All I want is for you to relax," he said, tapping the duvet apologetically. "Just forget what I said."

But Claire couldn't forget it. In fact she was thinking about his remark all night, turning from one side to the other. With only a few words he had planted a poisonous seed. It's in your head. Her head. Something was wrong with *her*.

Shortly after that they had an appointment with Miss Zelda, a well-known fertility guru in Harley Street. They had seen the brochures, pastel-coloured and clean. She looked like a secretary from an Eighties' film, with her high heels and a wide green patent-leather belt. Gently touching Claire's stomach, she said, "I can see it for you two. You will have a baby, believe me."

Her optimism was infectious. A diet plan was created. Claire would come in every week for alternating acupuncture and hypnosis sessions. Both of them were put on vitamin pills. Claire had to smile when she recalled Anthony's reaction, looking suspiciously at the bottle with the white tablets.

"It's to increase your sperm quality," Miss Zelda had said with a smile. "If you start taking it now, your next batch in three months will be excellent."

Claire was prescribed some Chinese herbs. She had to mix the gloopy greenish powder with water and drink it every morning. It tasted like glue. She forced it down although she always felt sick afterwards.

Claire finished her tea. She wondered what the woman with the twins went through to get her two bundles of bliss. On the way out the twins started to cry, both at the same time. They seemed to be spurring each other on, getting louder and louder as if in competition. Their cries filled the room and for a moment she wasn't jealous of the mothers, but relieved to be free to go.

She drove fast, skillfully zig-zagging around the

lined-up cars and buses of Marylebone Road towards King's Cross. Someone was hooting at her but she didn't care; she was in a rush. A part of Pentonville Road was cordoned off, as happened so often these days. Police cars, men in orange vests, police tape everywhere. Only last week when she came back home from work she saw two houses on City Road taped off, dozens of policemen going in and out of houses.

Claire drove through some back streets, going even faster now. She didn't want to be late, especially as Mrs Ross always seemed to be in a hurry.

They were already waiting for her in front of the gym.

"So sorry, the traffic –"

She started to apologise, but Mrs Ross shook her head. "Don't worry, I'll see you in an hour," she said, kissing Nora swiftly on her forhead and leaving. She was always dressed as if she was off to some glamorous event. Claire wondered what she was up to for the next hour, but of course that was none of her business.

"Are you up for a swim?" Claire asked in an encouraging tone, but Nora only nodded reluctantly.

Claire prefered one-to-one lessons, because the children who came to her privately did so because they had usually failed to learn to swim in a group. Nora was one of the most difficult children she had ever had to deal with – she was so afraid of water it would take a great deal of work before she would gain the confidence and to swim.

She took Nora's hand with a firm grip and went with her to the locker room. As soon as the musty smell of chlorine and damp swimming trunks hit her, she knew she was at work.

At this time of day the pool was almost empty. There were two swimmers in the fast lane and a couple of children splashing around.

"Do you remember the game we played last time?" she asked.

Nora shook her head, pressing her arm against her body as if to protect herself. She was clearly not in the mood for a swimming lesson.

Claire saw the woman instantly, triumphantly carrying her huge bump, the blue swimming costume stretched over her pregnant belly. Standing at the edge of the pool with her pale thin arms and legs, she reminded Claire of an octopus; there was something grotesque about it. The woman climbed down the pool ladder, carefully gliding into the water, and swam on her back with long elegant strokes.

Claire couldn't help but follow her belly, a little blue island floating up and and down the pool. She thought of the embryo in there, that was swimming too, in amniotic fluid. Nora had been there, in Mrs Ross's belly, not all that long ago and now she was here standing in front of her with her big brown eyes full of fear, shivering and trembling, seven-years-old and already a neurotic mess.

Claire talked to her in a low voice, almost whisper-ing, "I will carry you," she said. "Trust me."

She held Nora's back with her hands so she could just relax and feel the weightlessness of her body. "See? You're floating."

It was a way of familiarising her and making her comfortable in the water. She had to take away her fear of going under and drowning, the fear of losing con-trol. As Nora realised she was safe, she sent the signal Claire was waiting for: a little tiny smile. Her reward.

"Shall we try now?" They were only two metres apart, Claire standing there like a steadfast rock as Nora swam towards her, frog-like, in hasty awkward movements, her lips pressed together. "Head up," Claire shouted, "head up," and then Nora jumped. Claire almost lost balance as she leapt at her, legs and arms clinging around her.

"Don't let go," she stammered. "Please, don't let go." As her little face burrowed in her neck, Claire could feel the breath on her skin. The hot breath of fear. She stroked the back of her head, a reflex – was there such a thing as a reflex for affection?

The pregnant woman got out of the pool and, as she walked past them towards the changing rooms, she smiled at her as if they were sharing a secret. Maybe she thinks this is my child, Claire thought, maybe she thinks I am Nora's mother. At that moment she realised that this was exactly what it looked like.

Sadness struck her, overwhelming her like a crashing tidal wave. Pressing Nora's little dripping wet body against her, she didn't want to teach her to swim anymore; she wanted to leave the pool and instead buy her an ice cream, go for a walk in the park. There, sitting on a bench, she would calmly explain to her how important it was for her to be able to swim. Claire had always seen it as much more than just a useful life skill. Fear was the obstacle and impediment of any progress. That's what it was all about. Turning fear into strength and learning to keep her head up. With a sudden movement she broke away from Nora's embrace.

"Let's go," she said in a voice that sounded far more fierce than she had intended. "Let's try again!"

That evening, when they were sitting in their basement kitchen and Anthony was smoking his after-dinner cigarette, Claire told him about Nora the first time.

"It's normal to feel more affection for some children," he said, puffing the smoke through his nostrils. "Just don't get too involved."

Claire carried the dishes to the sink. Don't get too involved. It had sounded like a warning, and she loaded the dishwasher with more noise than necessary. The lightness she had felt after the hypnosis session had long gone. When they were watching TV later that evening, curled up together on the sofa, she didn't follow the story of the film. She was thinking of Nora and what her room might look like, how Mrs Ross would put her to bed. Would she read her a bedtime story, or just turn off the light and close the door?

*

Claire didn't know what to say. Of course she wouldn't mind. Quite the opposite. She was delighted to have Nora for half-an-hour longer, but that's not what she said. She looked at her watch as if to figure out whether she could manage it.

"You know, I don't have another lesson after this, so it shouldn't be problem."

"Excellent," Mrs Ross replied. "Of course I'll pay you for the extra time."

No parent had ever asked her to do that. If someone else had asked her, she almost certainly would have said no. After all she was a teacher, not a babysitter. But this was different. This was about Nora and she felt as if she couldn't say no to the extra time with her.

As regards the swimming lesson, it was by far the worst since they started a few weeks ago. It took her half-an-hour just to get Nora into the water. Shying like a nervous horse, Nora refused to enter the pool and when she was finally in there, she didn't move. She just stood there, shivering and scared. Hopeless. This is a

Sisyphus situation, Claire thought, one step forward, two steps back. This wasn't normal, far from it. Thinking of herself as someone with a lot of patience, she suddenly felt like she was about to lose it.

"You know what," she said. "Let's call it a day!" Nora looked suprised but utterly relieved.

In the changing room Claire helped her into her white cotton dress and matching sandals. The damp bathing suit looked limp and sorry; Nora quickly put in the plastic bag as if to get rid of the evidence of her failure. As soon as they stepped out into the sunshine, she sighed with relief.

They walked along Upper Street and Nora seemed another person altogether. She smiled at a little puppy that walked past. The torment in the pool was over, the world friendly and full of excitement again. How quickly the mood of a child could change. Suddenly Claire had the urge to treat Nora, to put the awful moments of the swimming lesson behind her.

At that time of day the cafe with the glass front overlooking Upper Street was almost empty. On display on the counter was a selection of luscious looking cakes, and Claire wanted Nora to have a piece. She chose a slice of the chocolate cake with the thickest icing on it, as well as a large lemonade.

As they sat on high chairs looking out at the pavement, Claire watched intently as Nora ate the cake at once, breaking it up with her fingers, bit by bit disappearing into her mouth. The slurping sound of the straw sucking up the drink reminded her of her own childhood, the hot summers in Berlin when her mother brought them freshly made lemonade in the garden. She and her sister Anne drank as much as they could, comparing their bloated bellies afterwards.

"Do you have any brothers and sisters?" Claire asked. Nora shook her head, putting the last crumbs into her mouth. "Nope."

A lonely only child, that's what Nora was. From that moment Claire knew she disliked Mrs Ross. Of course it was unfair; what did she know about them? Nothing. But there had been a coldness about Mrs Ross that had put her off from the very first time they had met.

"You really don't like swimming, do you?"

"Mummy wants me to learn. So she doesn't have to look after me on holidays. In Spain I almost drowned." She told Claire how she was playing in the sea, looking for shells when a big wave caught her by surprise. She got whirled around, emerging only for seconds, gasping for air before the next wave forced her down under again. "The man saved me," Nora explained. Claire noticed that she didn't say my dad, or even a name, just 'the man'. "Mummy was mad," she added.

Of course, she was too busy looking after herself while her child was drowning, struggling for dear life. Claire felt furious. There were so many questions she wanted to ask – where was daddy, for example. But she didn't want to come across as too curious. No wonder the experience had left Nora traumatised. However, at that moment Nora was here with her. Claire felt the urge to protect her, to look after her as if she was in danger, standing only an inch away from the edge of an abyss she was about to fall into.

"Can we go and see the angel now?" Nora asked, pushing back the empty plate and glass. It took Claire a while before she realised what she meant.

The Plaza was as ugly as any shopping centre, a U-shaped open-air complex crammed with shops. An elevator led to a mezzanine level with a cinema and restaurants.

Claire and Nora stopped in the middle of the square. There it was in front of them, the angel sculpture. Claire noticed it every time she came here to shop, overwhelmed by its sheer size. The massive silver wings on four spidery legs were spread out as if they were about to take off into the blue sky. The shiny stainless steel reflected in the sun. An iron angel. Towering over people going in and out of shops.

"Does the angel not have a face?" Nora asked.

"No, my darling, angels have no faces." She paused for a moment. Claire didn't know why she had said that. Angels have no faces.

"It's a bad angel then," Nora concluded quickly.

Claire looked at the sculpture. It was martial, warrior-like, as if ready for an attack.

"No," Claire finally answered, stroking Nora's head. "The angel is just fast asleep and that's a very good thing. It should never, ever wake up."

She took her hand. Nora didn't seem surprised at all and the gesture felt completely natural. Walking through the shopping centre, Claire felt strangely proud with this child at her side. Of course people assumed she was the mother, and in truth she didn't mind that at all. She imagined how she'd be at home with her. She would help her with her homework at the kitchen table and then they would prepare supper together. She would let Claire stir the pan while she would set the table for three – the comforting routine of everyday life. Later Claire would read her a fairy-tale from the Hans Christian Andersen book.

"Can you read it again?" Nora would ask and she would start again, and read until Nora was asleep.

It was Mrs Ross who woke her from her daydreaming. Claire felt reluctant to hand Nora over to her mother, who didn't even ask how they had spent the time. Claire watched their backs, and after a few metres Nora turned her head and waved at her. This image of Nora stayed with her for the rest of the day. Surely this gesture meant that Nora liked her. Why would she have turned and waved if she didn't like her? It was a sign in her favour. It must be. Children don't lie.

However, at home the house felt emptier than usual, the rooms bigger. Claire listened to the noises outside.

The steady brawl of the traffic of City Road, a dog barking in the distance. Only inside the house there was an inanimate, heavy stillness.

*

Her family was scattered all over Europe. Her parents lived in Berlin, her sister Anne in Hamburg, she had an aunt in Barcelona and an uncle in Toulouse. She kept in touch with all of them, by phone and e-mail, but it was Anne that she missed. Anne before the baby that is.

She had changed since she'd had the baby. It was something in her voice, an unfamiliar hasty tone. They used to call each other much more; now it was down to once a week. Often the conversation would break up, Anne would go away from the phone to give the baby a dummy, or pick something up from the floor. When Claire asked whether she should call later, Anne insisted she would be right back. Sometimes she heard Karl in the background, talking to the baby, making silly noises, or the beeping sound of a child's toy. Nowadays, there was always some noise in the background.

Gone were the days of intimate, sisterly conversations that could go on for hours on those lazy Sunday afternoons; the ones that involved several cups of tea and lounging on the sofa looking at the ceiling, talking about their childhood in Berlin, ex-boyfriends and rows, their weddings and other friend's weddings or the latest skin treatments, until they got hot ears or Anthony pointed to his watch, whispering, "You've been on the phone for over an *hour* now!"

Of course the subject of the conversations changed when Anne got pregnant. Anne would send pictures of clothes and toys to her mobile. Suddenly it was all about what colour the wall in the children's room should be and whether wooden toys have greater educative value than plastic ones. Sometimes Anne would tell her hilarous things, like when a man stopped her on the street, asking if he could please touch her bump because it looked so "delicously plump", or when she went to a baby class with Karl where they had to practise how to hold a baby properly on a life-sized plastic toy. Anne regarded this as a complete waste of time and "just pathetic", pointing out that the human race had survived for 200,000 years without such training.

Claire had been relieved to hear that Anne couldn't stand those over-excited mothers who suddenly start to dress like babies themselves, wearing bib overalls and pastel-coloured jumpers.

She also welcomed the fact that her sister wanted to go back to work as soon as possible; she saw it as a sign that Anne, even with a baby, would still be Anne, the way she knew her.

In the last days of her pregnancy, Claire called her almost every day. She was as excited and anxious as Anne herself, but at the same time grateful that she'd had the chance to see her sister going through all the stages of pregnancy. It was like when they were children, climbing up to that five-metre-high diving board for the first time and Anne, as the older one, jumped first so her younger sister could follow. There was something profoundly reassuring about a bigger sister who marked the route, always a step ahead, holding that particular thorny branch out of the way.

Claire and Anthony had flown from London to Hamburg a week after Anne had been given birth to Margarethe. It was their turn; all the family members came to visit one after another, the parents first then brothers and sisters, uncles and aunts. Everyone wanted to see the new addition.

Margarethe. An unfussy, solid name. Anthony didn't hide the fact that he didn't like it. Claire would never forget the row they had on the plane to Hamburg.

"It's a name like a rock, much to harsh for a girl."

His statement annoyed her. "What about all these silly flower names: Rose, and Lilly?"

"What about them? I like flower names."

"I don't, and I don't understand why English mothers try to be so original in finding new names. It seems a whole generation in England will be called after fruits and spices: Apple, Vanilla, Cinnamon, Saffron. It's just ridiculous."

Anthony had immersed himself in the in-flight magazine. "However, my daughter will never be called a German name. Margarethe. No way."

Claire didn't actually like the name that much herself, but his outright rejection had hurt her and she felt she'd had to defend her sister's decision. More than the name itself, she was pretty certain it was the fact that it was a traditional German name that he didn't like, but she didn't want to drag the row on any further, so kept silent until they touched down.

Anne's house was slightly set apart on a hill, near the Alster River. White and square with a flat roof, it was modern in an unassuming way. Anthony called it "the box".

Claire had anticipated that the arrival of a baby would turn everywhere upside down; she expected it to look like a storm had hit, but the only place where she could find traces of negligence was the kitchen, where the bin was overflowing with the empty aluminium packaging of ready meals.

Her parents had left the day before, but Claire could tell Mother had been there. The food hamper. Everyone else brought flowers. But it was food that was needed. Her mother knew that of course.

"They didn't want to leave; we literally had to throw

them out in the end." Karl laughed. "I was worried they were going to eat her up. Your mum was sucking Margarethe's foot."

"That's because newborns smell so nice," Anthony added.

"Like kittens, of straw and milk."

While they were all standing around the cradle, Margarethe was looking at them curiously. A toothless smile and a gurgling sound escaped her mouth. Claire took her hand and it clasped around her finger like a tiny buckle.

"She has your eyes," Anthony said to Anne. "As long she doesn't have my square chin I'm happy," Karl said, laughing. But Claire couldn't see any resemblance whatsoever. Margarethe looked like she had dropped from outer space and had just accidentally landed here in the cradle. She didn't really belong to this world yet; she still seemed more accustomed to the womb, to an altogether different habitat. Everything must feel so vast for a newborn, Claire thought. How cruel it must be to be born into cold, glaring hospital lights, fussed over by dozens of hands. How crueller still to learn that the story didn't begin with one's birth but much earlier, and that the storyline was set from the very beginning and there was nothing, not the tiniest little thing, a newborn could choose from.

Maybe it was that fundamental, frustrating fact of

life that made Margarethe produce the piercing cry that suddenly filled the room. Anne picked her up, offered her breast, but Margarethe refused, turning her head away from it, crying even louder, her body stiffening like it needed all its force to do so.

Poor Anne, she looked exhausted, tousled hair and all dishevelled, yet so happy, kissing the baby on its head with so much affection that Claire knew from that moment that this tiny crying creature was the love of her life. She cradled the baby, walking up and down the room until Margarethe nestled into the curve of her shoulder and her body relaxed again. Claire watched them, fascinated how mother and baby responded to each other in an almost invisible exchange of impulses, noises, movements and touch; a highly developed and complex form of communication.

"She will fall asleep any minute now," Anne said, putting her back in the cot. Everyone left the room and for a few moments Claire was alone with the baby. She looked at it closely, intrigued by its perfection. Suddenly she felt pride that her sister had produced this. There it was, the next generation. Maybe it was due to the fact they had the same blood running through their veins that she suddenly felt a strong sense of responsibility.

"It's alright, you know," she whispered. "It doesn't make sense to you yet, but eventually you will learn the names of things and with that they will get meaning. Just like a puzzle that is slowly being put together and will suddenly make a picture. Do you know why this Alexander Calder mobile that your mummy bought at a museum shop is dangling from the ceiling? It's because your mummy is an architect and she likes these kind of things and wants to pass it on. That is what parents do. They just pass on who they are. And this is where you are very lucky, Margarethe. You are safe. Your parents are good, intelligent people and you will grow up in a beautiful house in the best area of Hamburg. You really couldn't have chosen better, you know. So don't worry. Paddington Bear is sitting on the changing table over there, ready with his little suitcase patiently waiting for you, until you are old enough to take him on a journey."

Margarethe was now breathing in a slow rhythm, her chest rising up and down, her eyelids almost transparent, streaked with blueish veins, flickering in her sleep. What does a baby dream of? Does it dream at all? She looked at this tiny sleeping body, defenceless and completely unaware of its whereabouts. It really was as if she had just been dropped from the sky. Claire covered Margarethe with the blanket and, as if the darkness of the room was too much, left the door half open, leaving behind a triangle of light.

When Claire entered the living room they had settled with drinks on the anthracite-coloured sofa, looking through the floor-to-ceiling windows and out into the garden.

"Get yourself a glass of wine," Karl pointed to the bottle on the counter of the open-plan kitchen. Claire liked the sleek design, the slate tiles marking a border line between the kitchen and the living room with its floor dark maple. Everything was so carefully thought out. The cupboard doors in the white handleless space opened with the slightest pressure and closed silently. It was so much cleaner then her old wooden kitchen in London, with the knobs that got grubby in no time.

Leaning over the counter, a glass of Chardonnay in her hand, she followed their conversation. They were talking about Iraq. Karl held a strong opinion – he has always been against Bush but wasn't one of those who had joined the peace protests in Berlin.

"A lot of the demonstrators were just indulging in outright, dumb anti-Americanism. They are all wearing jeans, drinking Coca Cola and eating at McDonald's, blissfully unaware of how American and spoilt they actually are. What do they know about what life is like in a dictatorship? Nothing. It's easy to walk around Berlin or London shouting for peace, because you don't have to pay for it. In Iraq you would have ended up being tortured."

Anne intervened, but Claire could tell that she was just repeating something she had said before and wasn't really engaged or interested in the subject. She was simply too tired to get excited about politics or anything that went on beyond the walls of her house.

"I really don't think all 500,000 of those people who gathered in Berlin in the name of peace were half-baked students who just fancied a big party. Some of my friends went, too, and they actually had very good reasons." After her statement, Anne sank back, curling up on the sofa, putting a cushion behind her neck. Anne had that owl-like expression when she was going into sleeping mode.

"But Germany is in a special position anyway," Anthony said. "With their past they couldn't possibly be part of this war, or any war for that matter."

Claire walked over from the counter to the glass door, looking out to the rectangular pool. Anne had switched the garden light on.

"But Karl has a point," Claire said, looking at the perfectly still water in the pool, wondering why it wasn't moving. "Europe is awash with anti-American sentiment and there is something very phony about it."

Suddenly Karl laughed. "Why is it that Anne and Anthony stick together and Claire and I have the same opinion; it somehow doesn't seem right."

"I always suspected Claire had a crush on you," Anthony joked.

She looked at her husband and smiled. It was true that they often agreed on things. Karl's parents were diplomats, moving every four years, and Karl had spent his childhood in New York and all over Europe. Anne always said Karl was more European then German. Claire could relate to that. Apart from Anthony, they all shared a sense of rootlessness. Growing up in Berlin but born in Stockholm, Claire and Anne regarded themselves as neither German nor Swedish; they were European like Karl.

Anne, however, had always been very clear about one thing – she would have hated to be born German and had no reservation admitting it.

"What about Margarethe? She will be German, with that name anyway," Anthony said in response, looking at Claire with a squished smile.

"For Margarethe it will be fine because she is a new generation. She won't have that guilt complex."

"No, much worse, the poor thing will be living in a world overrun by terrorism. Besides, I don't have a guilt complex," Karl said, staring in his half-empty glass.

"That is because you didn't actually grow up here; you don't relate to the history that much. It also helps that you don't have any relatives who were Nazis."

Karl looked up. "You have a point there. A friend from work told me recently over lunch that he'd found out his great-grandfather was an SS officer in Bergen Belsen, responsible for hundreds of death. He's absolutely crushed."

"Well," Anthony added, leaning back on the sofa,

"my ancestors were probably involved in the crusades back in medieval times, killing innocents in the name of God. I'm sure somewhere down the line we are all related to some pretty grim people with blood on their hands."

Claire walked over to the bookshelves that covered the whole length of the wall. The upper shelves contained complete editions of Thomas Mann, Goethe, Hermann Hesse and history books. It was Karl's territory; Anne was more into art. She had a taste for expensively made art books with high-resolution prints. There was also a significant number of books about architecture she used for work. Claire recognised some of them, like the book about Palladio and his Italian villas that she had given her once for Christmas. On the bottom shelf were a range of home magazines and also a few copies of the magazine that featured Anne's house. It was presented over five pages as an example of a modern eco-home. They highlighted the fact that the whole house was powered by solar panels on the roof. The magazine had been circulated around the family and every member owned several copies. Everyone was proud of her. Anne, the brilliant architect. In their parents' house, the magazine was still on top of the coffee table.

Just when Claire wanted to turn away, she noticed something familiar: Hans Christian Andersen's fairytales. It used to be in their parents' house in the living room cabinet and she recognised the book immediately. The cover, with its ancient engraved letters, was worn from rereading, the cloth binding slightly loose. It was an old edition and as children they were not allowed to touch it. When Mother came into their room at night to read from it, sitting on the edge of the bed, there was always a special, almost ceremonial atmosphere. Maybe this was because the book was unreachable for them and its mysterious content full of adventures and hidden secrets. It was a fond childhood treasure, and it gave Claire a strange pang that this book was now here, in Anne's possession.

"Mum gave it to me so I can read it to Margarethe. If you have kids, I'll pass it on."

Claire turned her head. "Of course," she said, immediately ashamed of her feelings of jealousy.

She emptied the glass and slumped into the Charles Eames chair. Anne was watching her on the swivel armchair, turning around as though she were on a carousel.

"You know this is the only piece of furniture I still have from Berlin?"

"Of course I remember. We were living off pasta for weeks because of it."

Anne had spent a whole month's wages on it. The chair became the centrepiece of their living room. When they had shared their flat in Charlottenburg it was Anne who was in charge of the decoration. One of her favourite subjects was talking about creating a whole range of furniture on wheels that would reflect the new mobile and flexible way of living. The walls were white, and Anne forbade her to hang anything up. For her there was nothing more anachronistic than hammering a nail into a wall. "As long as we can't afford Mark Rothko, we will leave the white wall as it is. Why put up a crappy poster? A white wall is perfectly beautiful," was one of Anne's typical arguments and Claire never objected. After all, Anne did make the flat look special. She even had a way of arranging lemons on the kitchen table to make them look like an *objet d'art*. Right back then, Claire knew Anne would one day build her own house. She started spending her spare time building prototypes. The floor of her room was always scattered with perfectly built little cardboard houses. And here she was, in her own nest. Everything exactly the way she wanted it.

Claire stopped turning around on the swivel chair. Maybe it was the wine that had suddenly made her feel unpleasantly off-balance. She looked at her sister and realised how accomplished she was, that she had carefully planned this all along. Just like the flat they had once shared, the house was perfect. There was nothing obtrusive or too much. Everything had its place and purpose, without being overly minimalistic – even the concrete ceiling didn't seem cold. As she had dreamt in her student years, everything was mobile and neat. The coffee table was on wheels, even Karl's Brompton bike in the hallway could be folded together and carried under one arm.

Anne was now talking about her plan to start her own architecture firm. As soon as Margarethe was old enough to go into a nursery she would start drawing up a business plan. Karl was clearly proud of her intentions. "She is just not made to be an employee," he said to Anthony, lovingly rubbing Anne's arm. "She is too talented and thrives on stress."

Karl himself was quite happy to work for a company. As team leader of the web development department at a big publishing house, he had a very good job. Claire could see that he loved Anne and, more, he was proud of her. Was Anthony proud of *her*? She wasn't sure. It confused Claire that her sister seemed so complete and accomplished. When she got up from the chair she was still a little dizzy, blaming herself for drinking the wine too quickly.

"Are you alright?" Anne asked. At that moment Margarethe started to cry and, almost instantly, as if mother and baby were somehow invisibly wired, Anne hurried into her room. When they said goodbye, Anne holding Margarethe on her hips and Karl behind them, forming a perfect triangle, Claire embraced them dewy-eyed.

It was in the taxi on the way to the airport that Claire realised it would never be the same again, that with the baby came a distance that, no matter how happy she was for Anne, made her inevitably that little bit lonelier.

"Relax," Anthony said, moving closer on the backseat and caressing her as if he could sense her worries. "We will soon have our own little family."

It was this scene in the taxi that Claire remembered two years later, while digging holes in the earth. How convinced he had sounded, she thought. He couldn't then have anticipated how difficult it would be for them. She pushed the shovel harder into the ground, removing chunks of earth. It hadn't rained for over a week and the earth in the flowerbed between the patio and the brick wall was dry. They were having a barbecue and Claire had gone to the garden centre; now that people were coming over she had an incentive to do the garden. The flowerbed was only about a metre wide and she realised she had bought far too many plants and a complete mismatch of colours.

Overwhelmed by the enormous range on offer, she had just loaded up the trolley with whatever took her fancy. She went for strong colours as well as for names she was fascinated by, like freesia, ranunculus, salvia. In the centre they had looked promising, but in her patio they just looked displaced. Taking them out of their plastic pots, the bare roots dangling in the air, she felt a certain satisfaction putting them back into the earth, pressing the compost down and then watering it.

The year before, she had tried to grow flowers from seeds and bulbs. A complete failure. Not a single sunflower had grown from the seeds. There had been the odd cranky tulip but that was it. "Just don't take it personally," was Anthony's consoling phrase, though Claire couldn't help but feel that nature was somehow turning against her. Her body didn't work as it should and she wondered, as she looked at the dazzling display of colours before her, how long those plants would look like that before they started to fade away.

Anthony's face appeared behind the kitchen window. He waved at her; he always did that, even when he came out a second later.

"Sadie just called; she's coming a bit earlier," he said, embracing her from behind. "She wants to help me with the sangria."

"Sure, what do you think of the garden?"

"Very colourful," he said, holding her tight. The narrow border was so cramped with vivid yellows, blues and reds, a sea of colour, that it actually looked quite striking. She was sweating, covered in soil, her hands black from the earth. She said she was desperate for a shower.

"You can shower later," he said, pressing his crotch against her, teasing her earlobes with his teeth, giving her goosebumps.

"Sadie could ring the doorbell any minute," she said, knowing what he was up to but realising, if anything, it only made it more exciting. He pushed her forwards into the kitchen. She couldn't see his face but felt his fingers skillfully opening her trousers and undoing the hooks of her bra. Her body smelt of damp earth and salt. Looking down she could see the white skin of her breasts. The hard, warm flesh of his penis entering her from behind, she held on to the kitchen counter and listened to his moaning.

She welcomed this sudden outburst of passion. It hadn't happened very often lately. The whole baby-making business was quite a turn-off, especially as it didn't work. It was neither making love nor fucking; it was a third category altogether. An awkward mechanical meeting of two bodies for a very unsexy purpose. The hypnosis teacher had told her to visualise the sperm swimming up the uterus into the fallopian tubes. Claire couldn't think of anything less erotic. Miss Zelda had warned them it could take the fun out of it. In hindsight Claire thought that was putting it mildly. She should have been honest and told them that on the way to getting pregnant they might just get bored to death.

This time Claire didn't think anything and didn't care whether his sperm was swimming somewhere or just dripping out. Normally she would lie down on the bed for half-an-hour afterwards, a pillow propped up under her bum. On finishing, they didn't even look at each other; he just gave her a pat on her buttock and

Claire hurried up to the bathroom to finally take her shower.

When she came down 20 minutes later, her hair still wet, Sadie and Anthony were cutting up fruit. Sadie was standing at the kitchen counter, right where they had just sex; Claire wondered whether she had any inkling of that. Anthony certainly looked the part with his tousled hair and half of his shirt hanging out of his jeans. It was also the wide grin on Sadie's face that made her wonder.

"Hi gorgeous. So nice of you to have everyone over for a barbecue," she said, giving her a kiss on the cheek.

"It's called a window of opportunity. From next week it will probably be raining for the rest of the year," Claire said, popping a slice of orange into her mouth. Sangria. It was Sadie's idea. Since she'd been in Jerez on holiday she was raving about Spanish food. She had brought them sherry vinegar and chorizo that was still in the fridge.

"Where is Paolo?" Claire asked while pouring red wine into a big plastic bowl.

"Still teaching. He might come later. Why, do you fancy him?"

"Of course. Who doesn't."

Sadie always asked her whether she fancied her new boyfriends, and Claire always gave the same answer. It was one of their little rituals. Claire watched her cutting an apple into slices. Outlined against the evening sun, her shoulder-length auburn hair was glowing. A delicately crafted dragonfly charm was sitting in the little triangle on top of her cleavage. Sadie only wore jewellery from her own vintage shop. She was telling them about this actress who'd came in with a pug puppy and how everyone went "ahh" and "ooh, how cute" until the puppy lifted its leg, peeing on a 700 quid dress. Of course the actress paid the 700 quid, Sadie added, smiling. She'd had a good day. Since her shop appeared in fashion magazines she had a colourful clientele, from models to rock stars, and her shop had turned into a little goldmine.

Sam and Christine arrived. Claire could hear them parking their bike in front of the house. Peering through the lattice window to the street, she saw their feet on the pavement.

Anthony went upstairs to let them in while Claire rushed into the garden to arrange the folding chairs around the table; it would be light until late. She liked this time of the year around midsummer, when the daylight didn't give way but swallowed the evening hours. The windows and doors of houses were wide open; she could hear the voices of the neighbours. Everyone was out in their gardens and backyards. Soon their barbecue would be ready and the smell of coal and burnt meat would fill the air.

Behind the wall the neighbour's two little boys were

playing football. The soles of their trainers were squeaking on the paving, the ball smacking against the wall. Their mother was shouting something from inside. Laughter. Claire wondered what it was like being that mother, seeing her own boys running around, sweaty and red-faced. Their endless energy around her like something electric, something super-charged, something that made her shout and her voice sound out of breath even though she was probably just standing at the kitchen sink. A door shut and it suddenly went quiet behind the wall, as if a light switch had been turned off.

As she turned back to her own garden, they came, one after another. Sam and Christine were inspecting the area. "It's bigger then ours," Christine said.

"No, it's not; it's exactly the same size," Sam insisted. This was the kind of conversation Claire didn't know until she came to London, where every inch of property could be the subject of hour-long discussions. Questions like, 'How many bedrooms do you have?' were asked with the greatest interest and concern.

"Whatever, it's tiny," Claire said. "In Berlin you could have a mansion and your own cook for that kind of money." They both looked at her startled, like she had just snatched away a great opportunity from in front of their noses.

Anthony appeared, armed with a pair of tongs to

tackle the barbecue, and he had a concentrated expression on his face. It was as if they were still cave dwellers and he had just come back from a hunt, offering meat to his wife.

Sam gave some advice on how to cook the meat so it was still rare the way he and Anthony liked it.

"Must be a male thing," Sadie commented. "I never came across a woman who liked blood on her plate." She was pouring sangria into round glasses with a ladle. Maybe it was the ladle in her hand that made her look so wholesome and together, like someone who had everything she could wish for.

Claire wondered where it came from, that complacency. She had this strange feeling that Sadie was somehow carrying a secret. And it suddenly occurred to her, while she was fishing out an apple slice from her glass, that she actually didn't know these people all that well. All they really had in common was the fact that they were all in their thirties and forties and childless – maybe that's why they were all together there. Apparently like-minded people seek each other out, so they feel less alone. People were in fact just like sheep, gathering to keep each other warm. If they had children they would hang out with people who had children too, or not hang out at all, like their neighbours.

A light went on in the neighbours' house. It was the window with the Superman sticker on. She could hear the boys scream and she could just imagine them, jumping up and down on the bed, having a pillow fight, driving their mother to her wits' end. Wasn't she supposed to be that person, trying to get her children to bed? Instead of sitting here on the patio having a barbecue, desperately trying to enjoy herself, chewing on a dry piece of chicken breast?

As the evening went on, their voices got louder, buzzing in the mild silky air. Even though they were divided by brick walls, there was a certain communal feel that only happened in summer when the backyards and gardens became additional living rooms. Someone was laughing, a glass broke, Jack Johnson's soft, effortless voice came from a radio on a window sill: 'I hope this old train breaks down, then I could take a walk around, see what there is to see...' At dusk bats appeared, flapping over their heads. "Where are they coming from?" Sadie wondered.

"Probably from under the bridges on Regent's Canal," Anthony contemplated, his face unsharp in half-darkness.

Sam was rolling a joint. There was something childish about the way he was fiddling with Rizla paper, like he just couldn't help it. She had never understood his fascination with marijuana. It just made her feel sleepy and stupid. Claire didn't know what came over her, but she suddenly leaned forward and started telling them about Nora. That she went to that coffee place, bought her cake and how close she felt when she was holding her hand as if it were her own child. Relieved to be unburdening, she found herself adding, "I even imagined taking her back home with me."

Claire sensed immediately she had made a mistake. The words sounded wrong, desperate, like a confession. Everyone looked at her taken aback; there was a silence. She had changed the cheerful scene, the easy flow of the evening.

Sam shook his head, inhaling noisily. "Maybe you should have your own child to look after."

Claire didn't answer; she just looked at the empty bowl of sangria, the bits of fruit stranded on the bottom.

"I have read of women who are so desperate for a child that they steal babies out of prams," Sadie added. It was intended as a joke, but nobody laughed.

"I just did the woman a favour and played babysitter for an hour," Claire said, hoping to end the conversation. But it was too late.

"Why didn't you tell me?" Anthony asked, irritated.

"Probably because it's not that important," she said elusively.

For a second she contemplated making a scene; how dare he reprimand her like that in front of friends? Instead she decided to save her anger for later, shrugged it off and got up. "Tea or coffee anyone?"

"I'll help you," Christine said quickly, following her into the kitchen.

Putting the kettle on, she regretted her openness. Why did she have to talk about it?

"I can't believe he still does that."

"What?"

"Smoking pot," Christine said, pointing at Sam. They could see them from the kitchen window, the candlelight dancing on their faces.

"He promised to stop for good, you know."

"Sure," Claire answered absently, pushing down the plunger of the cafetiere, still feeling furious about Anthony's attack.

"We went to this information evening about adoption," Christine said suddenly, lowering her voice. Claire looked up.

"We have been thinking about it for a while... We did these tests and unfortunately Sam doesn't produce enough fertile sperm. Apparantly that happens quite often nowadays... According to the doctor, our chances of getting pregnant naturally are very slim."

Claire turned away from the window; she couldn't look at Sam – it was just too awkward to be informed about such intimacies, talking about his sperm while he was sitting there a few metres away, unsuspectingly enjoying his joint.

From the urgency in Christine's voice, Claire could sense that she had wanted to tell her this all along, probably waiting the whole evening for the right moment. She wished she could just hug her and tell her that everything would be fine, that she needn't worry. But she felt she would be lying.

Claire sat down at the kitchen table and told her how long she and Anthony had been trying to conceive. She could tell Christine now, knowing she would be feeling just as miserable.

"At least you have a reason why it's not working. The most frustrating term in reproductive medicine is 'unexplained infertility'."

"What is it then with you guys? Stress?" Christine asked.

"How pathetic is that," Claire answered promptly. "Stress is what woman in Third World countries have, struggling to get food and water."

"Maybe we have to accept there are certain things that can't be explained," Christine said thoughtfully. "It's hard though, when you see these women with their brood in tow, reproducing like rabbits, fat and ugly, shouting at their foul-mouthed kids on the street, and you ask yourself, why her?"

Claire was stirring her coffee. It was good to hear Christine talking like that. "I just never thought it would become such an issue, you know. I expected it to happen like with my sister. It seemed so easy for her, for most people it is, anyway."

Christine didn't answer but looked towards the lattice window; they could hear the tapping of heels on the pavement.

"But this is serious Christine. Adopting, I mean. Why don't you get donor sperm?"

Christine looked up, twisting her eyes and Claire realised that, as much it was a relief to talk, it was also painful and embarassing.

"That's what I suggested to Sam," she answered, whispering again, even though no one could hear them, "but Sam doesn't want to. He won't accept sperm from another man. He couldn't do it. And frankly, why do we need to have our own baby when there are so many out there in desperate need of loving parents?"

She was holding her cup with both hands, staring at it, frowning as if she was looking for an answer in there. "Maybe there is a reason, you know. Maybe I am meant to give a disadvantaged child an opportunity."

It was Anthony shouting where the hell were they that made them get up and join the others again. Serving the coffee, Claire looked at Christine when they were back outside, her short hair the colour of burnt caramel, the freckles around her nose, and she realised how pretty she was. Christine was laughing now, wrapping her arm around Sam, and it struck her how happy and carefree they looked even though there was so much emotional turmoil and heartache behind the facade.

Christine left just after midnight despite a chorus of disapproval. They would stay up into the night, moving their chairs closer to each other, and soon someone would go to the off-licence around the corner to get another bottle of wine. Sam would roll another joint, promising Christine it would be the last. At about two in the morning they would become hungry and start rummaging in the fridge for more food, finally cutting up the chorizo. Claire could just see these things happening like a film on fast forward, but she couldn't see herself there participating.

When she closed her eyes drifting off to sleep, she wasn't mad at Anthony anymore; she was just relieved that she knew at least one other woman with who she could share her pain.

*

It didn't surprise Claire that Mrs Ross asked her again, and this time she didn't hesitate to agree.

"Nora likes you," she said matter of factly. It was impossible to tell her age. Mrs Ross had a preserved kind of beauty, locked in time. Her smooth doll-like forehead suggested that she'd had some injections that had relaxed her facial muscles so they didn't move anymore. But whatever treatment she'd had, it was subtle and effective and didn't look over done. She was clearly a woman of taste, always dressed in expensive selected fabrics that accentuated her tall, slim figure. She oozed the cool, sexy elegance that men both admire and are afraid of.

"That's alright, Mrs Ross," she said, "it's a pleasure. But it isn't easy to teach Nora, I have to admit. She is very afraid of being in the water. I wonder whether she ever had a bad experience?"

Mrs Ross looked at her with surprise. "No, I don't think so; she is just very shy," she answered before rushing off.

It was the first time she had talked to Mrs Ross about Nora. Unlike other mothers, who asked eagerly every time about their child's progress, Mrs Ross didn't seem to care at all. To Claire's annoyance, some mothers would even wait at the big glass window and observe their children during the lesson. Mrs Ross was the other extreme.

This time Nora did as she was told. She glided into the water at once and even managed to do a few proper strokes, her eyes wide open, staring ahead with tightly pressed lips. She had clearly steeled herself for the lesson. Maybe Claire had finally earned her trust.

"You will get a reward for that," Claire said proudly, clapping her hands.

Back in the changing room, Claire contemplated going to a shop and buying Nora a toy as a treat, but quickly realised she couldn't do that without raising questions, and Mrs Ross would probably not approve of her buying gifts. She recalled the flyer that was put through her letterbox advertising a fun fair in Highbury Fields. It would only be a short cab ride away.

Nora was over the moon when she suggested they go there and maybe have a ride on a rollercoaster. "I wanted to go to the fun fair last weekend," she said, "but Mummy didn't have time. She's always working."

"And where is Daddy?" Claire asked curiously and cautiously.

Nora looked at her as if she asked a stupid question. "He doesn't live with us. It's only Mummy and me in the house."

They hailed a cab on Upper Street. It was strange to be in a cab with Nora; she could go wherever she wanted to with her, even leave London, and it occurred to her that Mrs Ross had entrusted her own child into her hands – into the hands of a complete stranger. It seemed irresponsible to Claire, like the fact that she had let her play in the sea in Spain even though she couldn't swim. How fragile a child was, so completely reliant on the decisions of its parents.

"That's where we live," Nora pointed out excitedly when they had got out and reached Highbury. There was something grand about the Georgian terraced houses fronting Highbury Fields.

"That's a nice area to live. Do you have a lot of toys?" Claire asked.

"I can show you," Nora said. Fumbling at the outside

pocket of her little rucksack she took out a key and dangled it in front of her nose with a triumphant smile.

"Our house is only five minutes away."

Claire was flustered. The prospect of showing off her house seemed to Nora suddenly far more exciting than the fun fair. She wanted to show off her room and toys and share it with her – now that she had a new friend. How attached she had become. It was flattering and worrying at the same time. Would going to her house be a step too far? For their own sake, they shouldn't bond too much.

"Don't you want to go to the fun fair?" she asked warily.

"Let's do it next week," Nora answered quickly, like she expected this to go on forever. She didn't yet realise that as soon she was able to swim their time together would end and they wouldn't see each other anymore.

"Please please," Nora begged, rolling her eyes as she sensed Claire's hesitation.

"Are you sure no one is at home? Your mummy doesn't want us to go to your house, you know."

"But she doesn't know, please please. Only five minutes!"

The house was in a quiet, leafy street. It was big, considering it was just the two of them living there. Claire envisaged an estranged well-off husband who had given them the house.

When Nora opened the door Claire felt like an intruder, stepping into forbidden territory. The spacious living room on the ground floor had the subtle emanation of wealth. An antique gilded mirror adorned the mantlepiece. The slim, tall Bang&Olufsen loudspeakers suggested a taste for classical music. Big abstract oil paintings were hanging on the walls, but it was the photos of Mrs Ross in the hallway and on the landing that captured her interest. They were professional pictures of Mrs Ross posing, smiling over her shoulder, or glancing to the side and showing her striking profile. Her face appeared in a multitude of expressions, some sultry and demanding, others pensive, almost fragile.

Claire wondered whether she was an actress, immersing herself in different roles like that. Nora's room was at the end of the corridor on the first floor. Through a crack in the door Claire got a glimpse of Mrs Ross's bedroom, a king-size bed and a stack of books on the bedside table. She was curious to know what Mrs Ross was reading, but didn't dare snoop around. Feeling guiltier with every step, she almost tiptoed.

From afar they could hear the noise from the fun fair and the screaming of the people on the rollercoaster. Claire looked nervously at her watch; she wasn't at all comfortable walking around this house, although she couldn't completely stifle her curiosity – it was also fascinating being in a stranger's house unobserved. Nora smiled at her, completely at ease, waving her into her room. It was spacious for a child's room, with a little dressing table and a desk with a little wooden chair.

Stuffed animals guarded Nora's bed like an army. "These are my friends," she said proudly. "I can only sleep with my animals around me." An array of teddy bears, birds and reptiles sat neatly lined up on the bed; there was even a snake curled up at the foot of the bed. A huge chimpanzee sat enthroned on top of the pillow like a guardian.

Nora told Claire their names, and she was intrigued by the girl's vivid imagination. Every animal had its set place in the hierarchy of Nora's Kingdom. She had even made up stories for every toy – she told her that she had found them on the bus or the tube, even in the garbage on the street, and that they had all been abandoned by their previous owners. Claire didn't believe that – they looked much too nice – but Nora seemed to believe her own made-up story. It was real to her, and there was something touchingly good-natured about the fact she saw herself as the saviour of the lost toys of London.

"That's very good of you, that you look after them, and give them your own bed as a home."

"Last winter he almost froze to death," she said, taking one of the numerous teddy bears in her arms. "Mummy said I have to get rid of half of them; she says I have no space in the bed for myself anymore, but I won't give them away. Not a single one!" she said decisively, clutching the teddy bear to her chest.

"Of course not," Claire agreed. "You have to look after them." She immediately felt devious taking the same line and undermining her mother's decision. Nora nodded, pleased with her reaction – she was a loyal friend, staying by her.

Claire could imagine Nora alone in her room, talking to her toys, playing games with the stuffed animals, mimicking their voices. That was the genius of children, the ability to bring everything to life, even a stupid mute teddy bear. What a shame, Claire thought, that she would lose this gift eventually, when she could read labels like 'made in Taiwan' and discover that the eyes of a teddy bear are nothing but hard plastic.

"I have something for you," Nora said, opening the drawer of her little desk. It was a crayon drawing of two stick-figures and an out-of-proportion angel with spiky wings.

"That's us," Nora said. Just as she was about to close the drawer, Claire saw something in there that was familiar – the golden dragonfly necklace that Sadie had worn at the barbecue. Claire reached out and took it from the drawer to have a closer look. It was without doubt the exact same necklace. "Where did you get that from?" she asked.

"I borrowed it from Mummy. I took it out of her jewellery box. I have to give it back, though," she said, looking down as if she had been caught red-handed.

"Give it back now," Claire said suddenly, in a commanding tone. As Nora left to do so, for a brief moment she was alone in the room. It was as if the stuffed animals with their dull empty eyes were disapprovingly staring at her, a stranger and intruder, standing there in the child's room, in the inner sanctum of the house, giving orders. It was then that she felt queasy and had nothing else in mind but leaving the house.

"We are going," she said, much too loudly. "We are going now!"

On the way home Claire almost had an accident. Driving from the gym in Essex Road back to Remington Street on a daily basis, she knew the route blindly. Lost in thought, she drove past the pub on the corner into Duncan Terrace, a line of grand Georgian town houses with bits of greenery in front. She always looked at them with some envy; she would have preferred to live in one of those houses, but they were considerably more expensive than the houses on their street, which backed onto estates of cheap council housing. She was now and again astounded how radically the scenery of the same neigbourhood could change. Just a few metres further down, turning left along Regent's Canal, the houses became more and more squalid. Nelson Place was a narrow street, flanked by shabby council flats, only a few feet long but always littered with beer cans and junk, smelling of pee as if it was an open urinal. Once someone had dumped a mattress, leaving it there to rot.

At night Claire avoided walking there on her own. She would go via City Road, which was better lit and busier, even though it was a detour and took five minutes longer. But during the day and on her scooter she didn't think it dangerous. As it was a one-way street and most of the time empty, Claire always accelerated to get through this bleak bit as quickly as possible.

A dog was scratching at the door of one of the flats, barking its heart out. But Claire didn't pay any attention. She was thinking of the strange coincidence that Mrs Ross possessed the same necklace as Sadie, when suddenly five or six children dashed out from a side alley into the street, shouting and howling, their arms stretched out, deliberately blocking her way.

She was forced to brake suddenly, before swivelling around, cursing. "Get out of the way, dammit!" she shouted. But they only jeered louder, showing her the finger. For a few seconds she lost balance, the creaking tyres leaving a long black mark behind. When she finally brought the scooter to a halt the children were gone. It was only when she was back in the house that she noticed she was shaking and her knees were weak and wobbly. The children probably came from the flats of Nelson Place or from one of the towers off City Road. It was somehow disturbing to know they were so close by, and maybe even knew where she lived. The neighbour opposite had his scooter secured to a tree with a massive chainlock, which until now she had thought excessively cautious. But maybe he had good reason.

Preparing dinner, Claire could hear Anthony coming down the street, recognising the distinctive sound his soles made on the pavement. His steps came closer quickly. He always walked fast. From Canary Wharf to Angel it took him just over 30 minutes when the tube was running smoothly, and five minutes from Angel, walking down City Road to Remington Street. She was relieved to hear the reassuring sound of his key turning in the door.

Following his invariable routine, he kicked off his shoes as soon he was inside and threw his Mandarina Duck working bag onto the sofa in the living room – the monotonous structure of day-to-day life, like the good bye and hello kiss on the cheek, the after-dinner cigarette or the sound of water filling a bath. After all that had happened, Claire listened to these noises like a consoling rhyme.

As soon as he entered the kitchen she hugged him

boisterously as if she hadn't seen him for ages, pressing her lips against his. However, from a stiffness in his movements she could tell at once he wasn't in a particularly good mood. Pouring himself a glass of Pinot Grigio, he mumbled something about his boss giving him a hard time. He never smoked before dinner and she was surprised to see him light a cigarette. Leaning back in the chair, pivoting on two legs, he blew smoke towards the ceiling. He closed his eyes and told her in a dark voice how the head of the department had summoned him to his office. Apparently he had projected the quarterly earnings of a pharmaceutical company much too positively and his mistake had lost the bank £600,000.

Claire looked at him. £600,000 was what their house cost. "Will you be fired?" she asked.

"No, but if it happens again I will be. Of course it won't happen again," he said angrily, hitting the table with his fist and furiously stubbing out the half-smoked cigarette. It looked like a broken leg.

Finally, over dinner, he told her about a particular executive who had let him down badly, giving wrong indications. But after all, it was his responsibilty, and this setback came as a huge blow. Anthony had hoped for a promotion the following year. When he started at HowlandRoberts he had told her excitedly about analysts who were highly ranked, treated like stars, who got huge promotions, and he had left her in no doubt that this was exactly what he was aiming for. He worked hard, getting up at six every morning and, at least twice a week, he called her from the office to tell her not to expect him for dinner because he was working late.

Claire admired his dicipline and ambition, and after his MBA and a Masters in Finance he had all the tools he needed for a career in the City. He shifted around the broccoli and carrots on his plate with a concentrated expression as if he was figuring out some complex mathematical problem, only half-listening when Claire told him about the near accident.

"They are just kids, fooling around," he said, playing it down as if she was making too much of a fuss about it.

"Fooling around? I could have hit one of them, or hurt myself. They're mean little bastards, Anthony, you should have seen the hatred they had in their faces. I wonder where that comes from."

For a moment they were silent, and the only noise was the scraping of cutlery on plates. Anthony looked tired. "Unfortunately, you'll just have to put up with it, because at the moment we can't afford to move to South Kensington, or even Duncan Terrace for that matter."

"I didn't suggest that we move house. I just told you what happened. Apparently we don't have the friendliest neigbourhood, that's all."

Maybe it wasn't the best time to talk about something delicate, but Claire had been waiting to tell him all along that Sam and Christine were thinking about adopting a child, and she couldn't hold back any longer. Anthony looked at her flabbergasted. "Well," he said, chewing slowly on a piece of steak, "if that's what they want to do, good luck to them."

"Is that all?" she asked. "I mean, why aren't we considering it? Since it seems we can't have our own children either."

"I would never ever adopt a child unless we had tried absolutely everything else first."

"But we have been trying for –"

"15 months," Anthony said and after a pause, "I want to reproduce." Claire smiled afflicted. How technical that sounded. 'Reproducing'. Like something animals do to sustain the population. "I want to pass on my genes," Anthony continued, "so something from me lives on, you know. Some people even say this is the meaning of life."

Anthony followed a clear path: the house, the marriage, a child, then a bigger house... the usual aspirations. And why not? After her accident, Claire knew she could never dance again and have a fabulous career like Anne, the award-winning architect with work in magazines. She saw herself ready to settle and have a family. But Anne now had a child... she had it all, and where was Claire?

"Just stop feeling so goddam sorry for yourself!" Anthony said briskly, getting up from the table. He had read her expression, that withdrawn, distant look again, which he saw as an indication she was brooding over all the bad luck she had. And how right he was, she thought.

Standing behind her, he slowly massaged her shoulders, a sign that his mood had changed, a familiar gesture that indicated he was calm and wanted her to be calm too.

"I can't help but think we still have a good chance, Claire. That the problem is something that hasn't been detected by the routine tests, something that could be overcome."

She knew before he said it. It was what she had hoped to avoid. The three letters had hovered over her head for the last few months like a fat black cloud.

"Let's try IVF."

"IVF?... but that's... that's expensive, invasive and... and desperate."

Of course she had considered it before, but had never really thought it would actually come to this. She never thought they would be one of those unlucky couples, and somehow she could still not imagine it. "Maybe we just need a bit more time," Claire added.

But Anthony was insistent. "No, Claire, we've wasted enough time already. And we are desperate. Or why is it then that you feel the need to bond with other people's children?"

"Nora, you mean?" Claire asked sheepishly.

"Yes, Nora."

She knew he was right. And it felt like a knife turning in an open wound. There was also no doubt that if Anthony knew what had happened that very afternoon, he would have been beside himself.

He finished the bottle of Pinot Grigio in front of the telly, watching *Friends*. With the canned laughter in the background, Claire surfed the internet, reading one horrific story after another. Miss Zelda had told her at the very first session never, ever to search the internet for the term 'infertility'. For a long time she had restrained herself, but now she was lapping it up, all the greedier for it. She read about clinics offering IVF – she was surprised how many there were – and the risk of multiple births. There were stories of woman with triplets, women who suffered ectopic pregnancies, ovarian hyperstimulation syndrome and miscarriages. One woman tried IVF unsuccessfully 12 times, and another died of internal bleeding during egg retrieval. Numerous in-depth articles dealt with the scientific phenomenon of the increasing decline in sperm quality. One doctor even warned that the sustainability of the European population was at risk, with every third couple being childless in the future. Apparently, she and Anthony were in line with the trend of a dramatically shifting demographic balance.

All sorts of dubious 'miracle cures' were advertised, from vitamin supplements and potions to herb juices promising to turn any woman into a baby-making machine if 'everything else had failed'.

A chat site offered contact with other women who were diagnosed with unexplained infertility. That's what the global village was also good for – sharing misery. Claire thought of an anonymous faceless crowd of women around the world, their nightmares and dashed hopes, deprived of what was universally seen as 'the meaning of life'. But in many articles there was also a strong undercurrent of judgement, that woman who left it too late have only themselves to blame. Childless women were either pitied for being cut out of the circle of life or, if childless by choice, judged as being selfish. In any case Claire got the message very clearly: she lived in a society that still saw the primary object of womanhood as becoming a mother. Childlessness was treated as either some form of madness or horrible disease.

'Childless? Welcome to the outcast' one website captioned. There she was, in the club of ultimate failure and anathema. And with the anger and sadness came fear. What if they tried IVF and it didn't work? What would happen to their marriage? She knew they would do it, but suddenly she felt an incredible pressure; what lay ahead was a sort of trial where she was on the table, stripped bare for everyone to see. There was no way out, like being forced to a near impossible task at gunpoint.

*

It had happened countless times before. Just as she pressed the buttons of Anne's number, the phone started to ring. Maybe it was telepathy.

"Claire?" Anne's voice sounded as clear as if she was talking to her from the next room.

"I was just about to call you," Claire said. "You beat me to it once more."

She imagined Anne, standing in the kitchen, her clothes stained with food and snot.

"How is little Margarethe?" It was always the first thing Claire asked now.

"Everything is interesting to her, the whole world one big playground. I just put her to bed, for her afternoon nap."

Anne wanted to discuss Mother's 60th birthday. Being the good daughter, she was always eager to organise a family gathering, trying to keep the family together, especially now that they all lived apart. Planing a surprise dinner party, she wanted her opinion on whether to book a private dining room at Borchardt's or Hugo's.

"Hugo's has a 360-degree panoramic view over Berlin and Mum has never been there," Claire argued. OK, that one was ticked off the list. Anne was babbling away about giving their parents a voucher for a round trip on a hot air balloon, from which they would have a bird's-eye view of chateau Sanssoucis, the Prussian Gardens and the lakes of Havelland. At that moment Claire changed her mind and decided she wouldn't tell Anne about their plan to embark on IVF, cautiously agreed on after their conversation the other night. It would only put unnecessary pressure on her and if it failed they would soon enough shower her with compassion, pouring their pity into her as if she were an empty, useless shell. 'Hope for the best and prepare for the worst,' was one of her former dance tutor's mottos that she had absorbed for her own life, and she decided that in this case it was indeed a good idea to prepare for the worst. Carried away by her own thoughts, she only half-listened, but suddenly her full attention was caught. Anne was reaching out into delicate territory, reminding her of calling home now and then. "They are asking about you," she said, emphasising the word 'a-s-k-i-n-g', as if to make clear that there was a profound lack of communication on her behalf.

Anne on the other hand was on the phone with Mum almost daily. Now that Margarethe was in the world, their first grandchild, they saw each other often at weekends in Hamburg or Berlin.

"You know, they're not gonna live forever." That was the sentence from the phone conversation that stayed with Claire for the rest of the day. Between the lines, wasn't this a rebuke, an undercurrent of, "hurry up with your offspring sister?" On past occasions, a patronising comment like that could have sparked a fight between them, but nowadays Claire just overlooked it, intrigued how Anne's side blows were skilfully embedded in a diffusion of well-meaning and apparent harmlessness.

"Sure. Will do," she replied, somewhat obstinately.

"And what about a birthday cake, something special, maybe tiered?" Anne continued.

"Whatever you say, Anne; you decide and we'll split the cost."

Anne's call left a sour after-taste. If she had meant to leave her feeling guilty and remorseful she had succeeded. It was true, of course, she rarely called home anymore. What could she tell them, anyway? There was no news.

After she had moved to London her relationship with her parents had changed drastically. They didn't approve of her going to London and leaving her job in the ensemble of the Berlin Staatsballett. For them it was simply a disastrous career move. Also, there were no friends or relatives in London, no connection whatsoever. They couldn't do the good parent thing and give her advice, not even an address or phone number. London just wasn't on their map. And maybe that was

– apart from what Claire saw as a 'necessary career change' – what most appealed to her. The experience of being in no-man's-land. Alone. It was her thing, and back then she was full of running away from home energy. Sure, she could have made it easier for herself by staying at the ensemble, like her parents suggested. But she was never the one to choose the path of least resistance. It felt right to veer off-course for once and be unpredictable.

She had a strong sense that that's what artists have to do, expose themselves, get out and leave the comfort zone; it makes them stronger, purer, closer to the core of truth; it refines them like a rough diamond, being polished by experience and loneliness. She wanted the world to wash up its driftwood on her. To go down under and come up again, take the plunge and swim. It was as much a mental exercise as it was physical, and she knew it was going to be hard.

"Why are you throwing away your talent and so many years of training and hard work?" her parents argued. But she didn't throw it away at all; she was just going to use her skills differently. After all, what was there left to achieve? Long gone were the days when she beamed with excitement and enthusiasm because she got assigned to the Berlin Staatsballett. It was a smooth transition from ballet school to becoming a professional dancer. Back then, there was never a moment of doubt that this was where she ought to be, on stage. And her parents made no secret about how proud they were of their two gifted daugthers. While Anne was ramming posts into the ground to build houses, she was pirouetting and flying through the air. Recalling her parents proudly sitting in the front row – they didn't miss a single performance, and often Anne would be there too, supporting her little sister – she felt rueful. It was those early years of performing that were by far the happiest. All she had dreamt of during her childhood and youth had finally materialised. She was in full command of her strong lean body, the product of many years of hard training. As soon as she went on stage she changed into someone else, someone untouchable, every movement a triumph of grace and beauty. After years of discipline she had finally overcome the profanity of the body; it wasn't just a peculiar machine anymore, eating and shitting and ultimately dying, a botched job, vulnerable and prone to thousands of illnesses. She had turned it into something else, into a perfect tool and medium. That was what ballet was – a smashing fist to the ugliness of the world. A fist to the terrible frailty of the human body. Ballet was for her the most convincing statement countering the unbearable imperfection of it all. There she was, united with the other dancers to create something that was better and truer than reality ever could be, combining symmetry, proportion and harmony to the highest level. Every night it reminded the audience that there was something grander then the trivial petty misery of their everyday lives.

'Beauty is truth, truth beauty – that is all ye know on earth, and all ye needs to know.' A fomer boyfriend she had danced a *pas de deux* with had stuck the quote on a Post-it note to the mirror of her dressing table. It was hammered into her mind as well as her chiselled body, marble-like and steadfast, like the column of a Greek temple.

At 26 her career as a ballet dancer had peaked; she had danced all the big choreographs, the *Nutcracker, Swan Lake* and *The Sleeping Beauty*.

However, although her bone structure was fine and elfin, she struggled to keep her weight down. More than once she was told to watch her weight and lose a pound or two, and with the years she found it increasingly difficult to stay within the limits.

Once a year she went on tour with the company, dancing in Japan, Russia and all over Europe. Although what had been exciting at first became exhausting and repetitive. After more then ten years of daily training, the evening shows left her more washed out than they used to. But what got to her most was the sudden, overwhelming loneliness after the applause. Sometimes she crashed into bed, sore all over, thinking of the many strained ankles and broken bones of the past years, the discipline and sacrifice, all the sweat, the travelling and failed relationships.

There had been dancers, choreographers and musicians, all men she had met through work. They were ambitious and full of energy just as she was, and it always followed the same pattern: after the physical attraction came the power game, and even when she tried to make it work it always failed, because ultimately their careers were more important. Too much hard work had been put in to give it up for so mediocre a thing as a domestic life.

Then, of course, there was the exhilaration, the passion of being on stage, performing in front of hundreds of people, the attention, the limelight; although the light was cold and harsh. That's what the dancers universally agreed upon – performing was better then sex, better then an orgasm and better then anything they had experienced. It was the one thing Claire missed most and found the hardest to accept, the fact that she would never be able to perform again.

During her last year in the company, the fights and bitchiness between the dancers started to get on her nerves. The competitiveness of the everyone-wants-to-be-the-best atmosphere, which used to drive her on, was suddenly wearing her down. Younger dancers appeared, ambitiously fighting their way up the career ladder, and dancers of her own age dropped out, settling down to have babies or become teachers in favour of a slower-paced life.

One of her best friends had to stop dancing for good

because, after years of jumping up and down on hard surfaces, her hip was so badly worn out that she needed a replacement. But for Claire, there would be another show, another night, another round of applause. Surely, with her willpower, she could have gone on for a few more years and maybe, with some luck, become a principal dancer.

It was around the events of September 11th 2001 that something changed. She had just broken up with a choreographer the night before. Anne had taken the week off to be in Hamburg with Karl and, without her, the flat they shared seemed big and empty. Anne and Karl had been going strong for several months and Claire sensed it was something serious. This was despite Anne having promised to never marry a German, as they regarded German men as unromantic. Once Anne had had a fling with a German who was completely silent and didn't even move his facial muscles when he made love to her. "It was like being with a ghost!" Anne had told her, horrified, when she came back home the next day. From then on, they always made jokes about German men being somewhat inept showing any kind of emotion, let alone passion. In the international surroundings of the company, Claire had had liaisons with Russians, Eastern Europeans and Americans. Morgan was a choreographer from Boston. He was 45 and madly in love with her – too much in fact. He wanted to take her back to New York where he had an assignment. In bed he was slow and peaceful, like a grazing cow. She liked his plump belly, the cosiness of his imperfect body, so refreshingly different from the hard, sinewy physiques of the male dancers who surrounded her. She could throw herself onto him, with plenty of space to rest her tired head, and sink into his soft consoling roundness. After they made love he used to smoke a cigarette and talk about them living together in a brownstone house somewhere in downtown Manhattan, surrounded by arty friends, having a fabulous life in Greenwich Village. Claire never responded; she was just happy to lay her head on his broad chest, listening to his deep voice and looking at the smoke rising, slowly disappearing in the air. However, his desire to take her with him became ever more insistent.

Finally, eating dinner at a cheap Italian after a show, the adrenalin still running high, Claire told him that there was no way in the world she would ever leave her job to live with him in New York. She looked at him, chewing on the limp crust of a lukewarm margarita pizza. With glistening eyes, he took her hand, stroking it as if he was saying goodbye to her hand rather then her. "You are too sensitive for all of this, you know," he said. "I really hope someone will make you happy one day."

As so often happened, it was a clash of interests that brought the relationship to an end. There was no row, no fight when they parted, just the sharp sadness that comes with letting go. But she would have no time to miss him, or anyone else for that matter, as the three months before Christmas were the busiest of the year. With every single show sold out, she would be on stage almost every night, dancing with a disciplined smile. Because she had worked the previous weekend, Tuesday 11th of September was a free day and she was supposed to give her body a rest.

Claire spent all morning in the bath, refilling it with hot water as it cooled down, thinking of Morgan and yet another failed relationship. Licking her wounds, she decided not to leave the house for the rest of the day. It was around three o'clock; she had just settled in front of the TV, watching *Tom and Jerry* and eating her favourite vanilla ice-cream with chocolate chips out of the tub, when Anne called.

From her agitated voice she could tell something was wrong, but when she switched, from Tom chasing Jerry, to the news channel, her first reaction was a fit of laughter. That must be some sort of a stunt, surely, what she saw could not really be happening. One of the towers of the World Trade Center was on fire. A huge pillar of black smoke ascended into the blue sky. It was a golden day in New York and it almost looked beautiful, like the graphic work of an edgy artist.

"Claire, this is not a joke, it's real," Anne said with

a grave voice. "An airplane flew into the tower. A lot of people died."

It took some time to take her words in. The presenter was looking increasingly nervous, as if he couldn't believe himself what he was reporting. "And I just received a message there is a second plane," he stumbled, and there it was, a white plane like a fast-approaching arrow, which crashed into the second tower.

"Oh, my God," Anne yelled into the phone. "What the fuck!" Claire could hear Karl in the background shouting. The presenter was stepping back as if he was suddenly thrown off balance.

"What's going on here?" Claire whispered, but Anne didn't reply. Even the presenter remained silent, watching as the massive explosion created a cloud of smoke of atomic proportions. In seconds, and in front of her eyes, the pinnacle of the world had turned into hell. Quickly, the presenter picked himself up again, delivering the news like pieces of a puzzle that he was keen to get completed. It wasn't just a horrible accident but an attack. Terror. That was the word that was used over and over again, delivered with a seriousness which made it clear that from now on people would have to get used to it. A word like a stab in the back. Terror.

"Do you remember when we went up there?" Anne asked with a battered voice. It was on a trip to New York with their parents, Anne and she were still children.

Claire remembered the big dark elevator that took them up to the Windows on the World restaurant on the 106th floor. It was exciting to be so incredibly high up, and a bit scary too. They were holding hands when they pressed their noses against the window, looking down at the Hudson River with the boats as small as toys. "Of course, I remember. You were scared because Dad told us that at that height the towers always sway a little in the wind."

Suddenly Anne shouted into the receiver. There was some movement on the top floor of the tower above the fire, but it took a moment for Claire to realise that those tiny figures were in fact people. She looked closer. Some had taken their shirts off, waving them like flags to surrender. Then they started to jump. It was bizzare seeing these people, as small and unreal as toy soldiers, jumping to their death, with the polished steel of the building behind them still and gloriously shining in the sun.

When Anne hung up, Claire heard the bleak dialling tone and looked anxiously at the phone. She was alone. Alone with these TV images, which were repeated over and over again. And then the tower collapsed; it just sunk into itself like it had finally had enough of standing there being stared at by the whole world. Claire held her breath; it was incredible to be watching this historical event in real-time, like an evil game just invented as a cynical new form of entertainment.

She was sitting at the edge of the sofa, the tub of melted ice-cream in her hand. She would be unable to do anything for the rest of the day, glued to the sofa as if she were watching a thriller. In some twisted and disgusting way, it was also terribly entertaining. But in order to bear it she was in desperate need of a stiff drink. She rummaged in the kitchen for that old bottle of single malt whisky that was still unopened – a souvenir from their parents of a long-ago visit to Scotland. 'Single Malt'. She read the golden letters on the label: something one was supposed to offer guests after dinner but then forgot about. It felt devious and completely out of character to pour herself a glass of whisky. Just when she sat on the sofa again, listening to a terrorism expert give a chilling analysis of the situation, her parents called. They were on holiday on a cruise ship. She had assumed that they were bronzing on a deckchair, blissfully unaware of what was happening in New York. But of course, the luxury liner had a high-definition plasma screen the size of a cinema.

Their voices came from afar; she could hardly hear them through the crackling of the phone line. The phone network was completely overloaded and it sounded like they were in some sort of a storm. "Stay home," they shouted. "I am home," she shouted back. As soon as she hung up, a peculiar silence unfurled. Everyone seemed to be sitting in front of the TV, the whole population of Berlin, Anne and Karl in

Hamburg, even her parents on their cruise ship, some-where in the Caribbean Sea, were watching the twin towers collapse. Everyone was connected by the same images, simultanously taking in the same information, mysteriously bound together by these attacks that until that day had been unimaginable. This was new, in scale and impact, and targeted at the very heart of modern society.

At first she tried the whisky in tiny sips, the sharp taste burning her throat. Gradually it became smoother. A deep warming sensation ran through her body as though someone had wrapped a blanket around her. As the full scale of the atrocity slowly unfolded, she remained transfixed to the screen. She couldn't break away from it, as if the screen were a big magnet in her living room and she was forced to take in everything it showed. It was people's crumbling faces that were the most disturbing, the collapsing twin towers mirrored in their panicked, wide-opened eyes.

She saw people running for their lives, covering themselves from the plumes of smoke worming their way through the streets. Downtown Manhattan was drowned in debris and ashes. Terrified people were screaming, crying, some were holding their heads in their hands as if they wanted to screw them off so as not to see, not to witness. A man in a suit with a brief-case was completely covered in ash. There was even ash on his eyelids. He looked confused, shouting into the camera, indecipherable sentences as if he had lost his mind.

Now she was drinking the whisky in big gulps. Maybe it was its numbing effect, or perhaps she had seen too much already, with the attack on the Pentagon and the plane that crashed in a field in Pennsylvania failing to trigger the same harrowing effect. Compared to the other two attacks, they seemed almost negligible, an afterthought. By late afternoon Claire couldn't move anymore. She muted the TV and, lying there on the sofa drunk and heavy, she fell asleep.

Shortly after midnight she woke up. A parching thirst made her open her eyes. Her tongue was clinging to her palate. But as soon as she tried to get up, she was so dizzy that she had to sit down again. It was dark. Only the blueish flickering light of the TV filled the room. She held her head; a headache was creeping up her neck and would soon burst into a full-blown migraine.

She couldn't believe she had let herself go like that. She stumbled to the toilet as fast as she could. Embracing the toilet pan, she vomited violently. Lying on the cold bathroom floor, her body deflated and completely powerless, moaning and weltering from one side to the other, waiting for the next sick wave, she knew there and then that something had changed profoundly.

It wasn't just a building that had collapsed in New York. She recalled the image of the falling people and imagined what it looked like when they hit the ground. Men in white shirts and ties. Men who looked like her father, or the waiter in the Windows on the World restaurant who had given them the Coke with a pink straw in it. "Now that's a view! You are lucky girls, it's a golden day today."

She remembered him saying that. A golden day. Slurping their Cokes, they looked down the Hudson River in awe. How beautiful it was. The little boats crossing the blue. Later on that day they were on a boat themselves to Liberty Island. There she was, the woman in blue-green copper, standing on a stone pedestal in the form of a star, holding up the torch. Her right foot raised, trampling on broken shackles as if she was about to walk forward. Inside the Statue of Liberty she followed Anne closely, going up the narrow, winding staircase, some 300 steps.

"We are in her head," Anne said. It was fascinating, being inside and walking around the head of the Statue of Liberty. For them, New York was just one huge playground. That's what the Americans were so good at – creating the illusion that everything was just some sort of toy, even a huge, ruthless city like New York.

Claire's stomach churned painfully. Although it was empty and all fluids squeezed out of her, there was still the urge to vomit, with nothing left apart from bitter-tasting foam. For a moment Claire thought she might just die there of alcohol poisoning on the bathroom floor. She tried to remember how much she drank. Two thirds of a bottle – was that enough to die? Her forehead was cold but sweaty, shivers went through her body like electrical currents, just as she imagined suffering from malaria would be like. She closed her eyes, her parched lips half open. Claire didn't know how long she lay there but, when she returned to the living room, she could already see the light of dawn creeping in.

The alcohol had knocked Claire for six and, because she wasn't used to it and had literally flushed her veins with a toxic substance, she had a hangover for almost a week. She felt sick throughout, cursing herself for her weakness. She didn't tell anyone, not even Anne, and did everything not to let on. But it was as if she was oozing the smell of alcohol from every pore. The faint taste of whisky remained on her tongue for days, and she had to force herself to eat. She was surprised and disappointed that her body, a perfectly designed dancing machine, had collapsed so easily.

Even in the ivory tower of the ballet academy everyone was talking about what had happened in New York. Everyone seemed to know someone who knew someone who was injured or killed or missing. There was an atmosphere of disbelief and outrage. 90 countries had lost people. Every day new bodies emerged form the rubble, as did new stories of missing people. Soon the faces of the terrorists appeared on the front pages. Somehow she had imagined old, bitter men. But they were young and didn't look particularly mad or stupid or suicidal. Although, what was a terrorist supposed to look like?

Outrage spread through Germany when it emerged that Mohammed Atta, the ringleader of the hijackers, had in fact lived in Hamburg. In Marienstrasse. The most unassuming of street names. The fact that the terror attack of the century had actually been planned in a room of the Technical University Hamburg-Harburg made it even more disturbing. Especially as Anne knew the place well, having once been to a seminar and having friends studying there. Her phone was ringing frantically; everyone wanted to know whether she had ever met him. She hadn't. "Maybe I passed this guy in the cafeteria or the hallway, you never know. He could have been one of those nerds who don't look you in the eye because they are full of thought and on a mission, but usually they want to build stuff, not blow it up."

It made Claire sick that her sister may have encountered such a terrorist, or even that she had walked through the same building. There were no boundaries anymore; the world had shrunk to an inextricable wireball, everything was linked up and anything could happen anywhere.

On the S-Bahn, she started to look at people more closely. One evening, only a week after the attacks, Karl had visited for the weekend and he and Anne had had an argument.

Anne confessed that she had actually left a train because of three young men who had reminded her of the suicide bombers she had seen in the papers; they were whispering, and she thought something fishy was going on. "Next they'll probably blow up the trains," she said.

However, Karl argued that this is exactly what they wanted, to spark fear and distrust, and ultimately to divide people. He thought it paranoid to leave a train just because someone might look suspicious and accused Anne of being judgmental, which she thought outrageous. Claire could sense that they were on the brink of a full-blown fight and left the table, but the air remained highly charged the whole evening.

In the week after the attacks a number of controlled explosions were carried out at train stations and airports around Europe. Claire had a dull apprehension that this wasn't it, that something worse was still to come. If causing angst and confusion is what the terrorists wanted, as Karl had said, they had certainly succeeded with her.

Politicians meanwhile were quick in urging people to go back to business as usual. This was exactly what the ballet company was doing. The shows went on uninterrupted and the curtain went up every evening. It was as if there was a sigh of relief in the audience, relief that on stage there was still this intact perfect world. Princess Aurora fell asleep before she got kissed to life again by the prince so they could get married for the umpteenth time. Stripped bare of the dancing, the storyline of *The Sleeping Beauty* was silly, and it amazed Claire that it had still worked every time since Tchaikovsky wrote it over a hundred years ago.

Watching the dancers warming up for a dress rehearsal one could think the world was indeed a wonderful place where beauty was truth, truth beauty and this was all we know on earth and all we need to know. Claire took the Post-it with the quote from the mirror.

"The world is fucked; what are we dancing *The Sleeping Beauty* for?" Claire said to a fellow dancer getting into her fairy costume. Suddenly it felt so pointless, even ignorant. What was she doing here, graciously hopping around in a tutu? The answer was persuasively simple, and the fairy delivered it so drily that she was taken aback. "We are here to make people happy, Claire."

On stage she slipped into her alter ego; she left the worrying Claire with the bad hangover in the changing room and transformed into Claire the dancer. She could feel her muscles tightening and her feet followed the sequence of steps as if of their own accord.

Swishing forwards and backwards in a pendulum movement, the supporting leg straight, she glided effortlessly from one position into another. Preparing for a leap, she bent her knees for a grand plie, her back perfectly aligned with her heels and her legs turned out. With the front leg sweeping forcefully, she performed the splits in mid-air in one fluid movement. Every limb reaching out, she felt her old self again. She didn't have to think about it, her body just did what it was trained to do, and for a moment she forgot everything else. It was in those moments, when she was completely immersed, connected with the other dancers through their simultaneous movements, gliding over the floor and jumping through the air, that she felt most alive.

Just as she was in a particularly difficult position, holding arabesque, her leg at a 90-degree angle, she heard Miss Clark's voice shouting, "Get your leg up, Claire!" and in a commanding tone, "Higher!" It shattered her confidence immediately. For the rest of the rehearsal she was out of sync. Like a discord in a piece of music, she created a disharmony in the group.

Suddenly she forgot steps, the lightness disappeared and with it the smile on her face.

As an acclaimed former principal dancer, Miss Clark had no mercy. Back in her heyday she had famously danced the Black Swan. She was perceived by her students as a living legend and her training was notoriously strict. Not even the tiniest slip escaped her eagle eye. One of her practices was to hold a burning cigarette close to the thigh so the terrified girl would get her leg as high as possible.

At the end of class, Miss Clark took Claire aside, asking what was wrong with her. Claire admitted having nightmares since the 9/11 attacks and problems concentrating. "Have you lost anyone?" She shook her head. "So, what's the problem then? Why does it concern you so much? We have no time for problems like that, Claire. If you need to see someone, then go and see someone, but don't bring your personal problems into class. You have to compartmentalise, you know? That's the only way to stay focused and professional. You can't let world matters affect you like that."

Of course there was no such thing as taking some time off at the ballet company. If she left for just two weeks she would be out forever. There were plenty of aspiring dancers out there waiting to take her place.

When Anne informed her the same evening over dinner that she was leaving Berlin to live in Hamburg with Karl, it was a slap in the face. Anne's decision to live with Karl was hardly surprising, anyone in the family had seen that coming, but somehow Claire thought Anne would never do that to her, leave her in Berlin on her own. In her imagination they were inseparable. The two sisters, a perfect item. No man before had ever had the power to come between them. But with Karl it was different. "Don't look like that!" Anne said. "We will visit. It's not like we're not going to see each other anymore."

It hurt. Claire smiled with pursed lips. The parts were cast and she just happened to get a minor role in a film she didn't even want to be in. It all coincided. The terror attacks, Anne's decision to leave Berlin and her fading enthusiasm for ballet. Everything she'd built was falling apart quickly and she felt unable to stop it.

In hindsight, it was only by chance that she had opened the e-mail an old friend from ballet school had sent her. She suspected one of those impersonal e-mails containing jokes forwarded to a random list of friends, something she normally deleted immediately. She knew, however, that her friend was involved in theatre and liked quirky perfomances that weren't mainstream. Once she went to see a performance she had choreographed, which, in Claire's view, was a complete mess and on that evening had made her mind up that she wasn't into experimental dance; Claire saw it as a synonym for mere lack of skill.

Therefore, when she clicked on the link, she expected some strange, edgy stuff that would at the best amuse her. But to her surprise she was immediately captivated by what she saw. A group of dancers were throwing themselves to the floor, crawling forward and suddenly flipped backwards. Then, they were spinning on their heads, before jumping through the air, light and effortless as if flying over the stage. In a sudden change of rhythm, they were moving in slow motion, trying to get out of an invisible net, in the next second they backflipped and walked on their hands, making their bodies look like they were made of rubber. It was the dynamic of their movements that was most arresting. Highly skilled, they mastered all the different dance forms. Merging elements of ballet, modern dance, acrobatics and breakdance, using every single muscle of their bodies, they created something that was beyond boundaries, something completely new. A dance like an attack.

Claire had never been particularly interested in contemporary dance, but this performance was a revelation. Compared to classical ballet, with all its rules and limits, this seemed like a huge liberation. Engrossed, she searched the internet for everything she could find about them, and came across similar dance groups and dance schools, most of them based in London.

Berlin had changed or maybe it was her, looking at the city differently. Everyone was raving about how international and open Berlin had become, but to Claire the city felt suddenly constricted. As she slogged along, she dreaded the day Anne would move out and leave her behind.

The house-warming party of one of her colleagues came as a welcome distraction. Iris had an unusual and refreshing number of friends who were not dancers. Normally, dancers only mixed with dancers and Claire was looking forward to talking to people who had nothing to do with ballet. A friend of Iris was DJing in the living room. A chandelier was hanging from the ceiling. Even if young Berliners didn't have any furniture, for some reason they would always have a chandelier.

The spheric sound of Goldfrap, and Air's *Moon Safari* filled the enormous white painted rooms. Iris had knocked down several walls. Knocking down walls and making big apartments even bigger also seemed a favourite pastime of Berliners. Almost everyone was renovating – at the party Claire saw several people with paint on their hands. Iris lived on her own and had three bedrooms and two bathrooms which were now cramped with people drinking Corona beer and cheap white wine.

A man in his mid-twenties with fair hair staggered in her direction. "I really want to fuck you," he said, a strong smell of alcohol escaping his mouth. Sweeping away his blonde fringe he looked at her as if he had just offered her something truly amazing.

"That's very funny," she replied, stepping away from him. But in a sudden aggressive gesture he grabbed at her elbow, leaving a red mark on her skin.

Without another word he went to the dancefloor where he made some grotesque moves, almost tumbling over.

Claire was rubbing her arm, hoping he would bang his head on the floor, when she overheard someone say, "My friend just came back from New York. A bit of rubble from Ground Zero is now more expensive then a piece from the Berlin Wall. They sell the stuff in little plastic sachets like cocaine."

Claire turned around. The voice belonged to a small man with a nose ring and leathery skin. He looked like he had spent too much time in the sun. The woman he was talking to was very slim; Claire suspected she was a model. There was a hint of a nod and the tiniest of smiles. "The nice thing about dancers is that at least you know they shave," she said, completely ignoring what had just been said.

Claire had had enough. She was just about to leave when someone slapped her on the shoulder. "Are you always just drinking juice?" a man with an Italian accent asked, and offered her a glass of wine. Claire explained she was still recovering from a bad hangover. "The best way to overcome a hangover is to drink even more," he insisted.

Claire took one of his cigarettes. It tasted good with the wine. Enzo. She liked his name. He was a photographer. When she asked him what he photographed, he said dismissively, "fashion stuff". She told him she wasn't particularly happy with her job either.

"Maybe it's time to change," he said.

"It sure is," she replied, and drank the wine in big gulps.

They left together. On the way out she saw the blonde man sunk to the floor, sleeping. People were stepping over him like he wasn't there. In the cold November air, their breath formed white clouds.

"I'm starving," Claire said, suddenly feeling ravenous. Following the blinking light of the TV tower, they walked towards Alexanderplatz. Enzo knew a kebab place, "the best in town," he promised. The square was empty, except for a lonely drunk, kicking an empty beer can as he staggered along. At the kebab stand they both watched with hungry eyes the knife slicing the brown meat. Claire could feel the heat from the grill on her face. In that very moment she knew she would spend the night with Enzo. A consoling thought, and she knew he knew it too. Glances, miniseconds of movements, the way he removed a breadcrumb from her lips, all that was just a confirmation of their mutual agreement. There was no need to talk, no words were required, and she was surprised how straightforward and uncomplicated things between humans could be.

Enzo lived in Wedding. She had never been there before, but she heard it was a shithole. It was the last S-Bahn stop and they were the only passengers in the carriage. He took her face in his hands and opened her mouth with his tongue. From the corner of her eye she could see their reflection in the window opposite. She saw a kissing couple who could have been together forever.

He lived in a huge loft in an industrial no-man's-land. In a gentlemanly manner he took her hand to walk over old railway tracks covered in weeds to get to the factory-like concrete building. He lived in one room, big enough to bicycle from one side to the other – his studio and living place in one. Claire couldn't take her eyes off a big photograph of three naked women in high heels. They were walking towards her with a fearless expression, as if there was nothing in the whole world that could hold them back.

"Helmut Newton," Enzo shouted from the other end, where he was cutting up a lime for two gin and tonics. "He is my hero."

It was right there, in front of Helmut Newton's three woman where Claire circled to the floor. She heard his steps coming closer. Good leather shoes, she had noticed earlier. Excellent taste, she thought. She looked up and saw the top of his head. It looked like his head was part of her body, completely embedded between her legs. His tongue flicked between her labium, then he kissed her clitoris, caressing it and sucking it gently. 'Why not,' she thought, and closed her eyes. 'Why not'.

The next day she called Miss Clarke, telling her she had a bout of flu. It felt like truancy. She just couldn't face going to training, let alone on stage. Maybe it was because she wasn't supposed to be there that she walked along Kurfürstendamm in such a pleasantly relaxed mood, like a stranger, someone who just happened to be in Berlin for a short visit.

She looked at the Kaiser Wilhelm memorial church with the snapped-off steeple. A family from England was standing there looking at the bombed facade. The father explained to his two young children what had happened there 65 years before. They looked at him as if to say, why should we care what happened such a long time ago? Claire could tell they just resented every minute of this excursion through Berlin.

"65 years is nothing," the father said into their bland faces. "If you consider the age of the planet, it has only just happened. In relation to the universe a lifetime is absolutely nothing." Claire was tempted to add, "And you two little shits are just two more farts on this planet – although you think you are so much more than that."

Claire stood there feeling sorry for the father, who was smart enough not to put his kids in one of those stupid tour buses for tourists, where a man on a microphone with a heavy German accent would bury them in names and dates. He had actually bothered and made a real effort to give his impervious brood an idea of Berlin's past. For a moment she wanted to hug him for his worthy attempt and to tell him that the intellectual decline of the next generation really wasn't his fault.

Later that day she lost herself at the KaDeWe. In the dim light of changing rooms, trying on more and more clothes, it was like building a bird's nest in the little cubbyhole, a perfect hiding place. Time stood still. Far away her colleagues were sweating away, stretching their limbs.

Enzo left a voicemail on her mobile phone but she didn't reply. It had been a perfect encounter; there was nothing to add to it. Getting to know each other would almost certainly just turn a good memory into a bad one. This way Enzo would forever stay a perfect image, a moment frozen in time and, unlike her previous relationships, with no story and drama to ruin it.

It was already dark when Claire walked towards her house. For a little while she just stood there, on the opposite pavement, looking up at their window, a square of light. She put down her bags and realised she had bought almost all the clothes for Anne. For a short moment she saw her slim silhouette in the window frame, a scurrying shadow, and at that moment she knew; she was about to leave too. She had bought farewell presents.

The news that she was going to quit her job at the Berlin Staatsballett spread through her family like wildfire. Her parents called a crisis meeting in their home in Grunewald. Even Karl was there; he was now considered part of the family, with the expectation that he would soon propose to Anne.

It turned out to be the most unpleasant dinner Claire could possibly have imagined, and it ended with her leaving in tears, slamming the door behind her. No one seemed to understand or accept her decision. Her mother called her selfish and accused her of being completely blind, quitting such a prestigious place as the Berlin Staatsballett without an equal offer at another company. Her father couldn't believe she wanted to go to London. "What is my daughter going to London for? Why can't you go to a nice place like Paris, an elegant city at least, where we have friends?"

Most disappointing was Anne, calling her stubborn and immature. Only Karl seemed to understand, adding, "Sometimes you have to take risks in life." But Anne looked at him fiercely, clearly saying 'shut up!' and, not wanting to lose his recent rise in the family hierarchy, that's exactly what he did.

Later that evening, her uncle from Toulouse called, trying to talk some sense into her. "Think of your parents, all they have invested, the excruciatingly high fees for ballet school."

It took all her strength to stumble the words into the receiver. "Yes, but I am not some sort of investment. I think I am allowed to do what I want with my life."

Maybe she was just following a centrifugal force. She would have to find a new place, a life without Anne, a life without the limelight of the stage. She would go to a new city and learn other moves, other rhythms. Meet people with different names, talking in a different language. She was running on high adrenalin, keen to get out of the flat before Anne. She managed to get everything organised within two weeks. All she could feel when she took off from Tegel airport into the clouded German sky was the excitement and fear of going on an adventure.

*

Miss Zelda looked at her with a faint smile. Her disappointment was palpable. "I hope you will be strong enough for this, Claire. Some people say IVF is the most gruelling experience."

Claire swallowed. It was as if she had betrayed her, moving on to 'mainstream' medicine. In Miss Zelda's eyes she was a failure. Slowly shaking her head, she closed her file. "Good luck," she said, and opened the door.

This time Claire didn't look at the photos. All the smiling mothers were hanging there on the wall like trophies. Supposedly the evidence of Miss Zelda's success. But she wasn't part of it. At the reception Claire paid her last bill. The receptionist swiped her credit card with a bored expression. She tried not to think about the amount of money they had spent on all the alternative treatments in the last few months. But more than the waste of time and money, she felt robbed emotionally. It was as if she had let Miss Zelda down – especially as she had seemed so optimistic at first, seeing her as one of her hopefuls. Of course every patient who left without being pregnant was ultimately bad for the reputation of the clinic. It was a business, after all, and the babymakers of London were in fierce competition.

Only a few days earlier the most successful IVF clinics had been listed in *The Times*. Anthony didn't hesitate and made an appointment with the clinic with the highest success rate.

"If it doesn't work, at least we know we've tried everything we could." He was right, but it was little comfort.

Claire went to Paul for the last time. Her little ritual had come to an end. This time the cafe was almost empty. Chewing a French Danish, she contemplated the term 'unexplained infertility'. What a strange name for a medical condition. How was it possible to do all those incredible things – flying to the moon, searching the depths of the ocean for new species, but not explain what the hell was wrong with her, not being able to do the most basic thing in life, to conceive and reproduce? Once her body had been her friend, a reliable source of pleasure and pride. Now it had turned into her biggest enemy. Above everything, she was angry. Why was her body letting her down like that? It had a problem that didn't even have a proper name! Unexplained. What a scam. She had done everything: massages, hypnotherapy, acupuncture, stuffing herself with healthy food. Still her body was defiant. She would almost have preferred to have some terrible medical condition that would explain why she couldn't conceive. At least she'd have an answer, something that would be much easier to accept. Carrying a womb in her body appeared just pointless. Especially as everywhere around her was nothing but mindless procreation.

Claire put the lock of the scooter into the compartement under the seat. Since the incident with the children she had bought a new chain, one that was heavier and more difficult to cut. A day after the near-accident someone had scratched the word 'cunt' into the white paint of her scooter. It was just petty vandalism, but it still made her look over her shoulder as she parked it.

On Euston Road she noticed the Gothic red-brick facade of St. Pancras hidden behind scaffolding; many buildings in the area had been cleared for demolition work. Cranes were slowly moving their long necks, like giant birds picking at the earth. They were working to improve the Channel Tunnel rail link – soon people could get to Paris in just two hours. The whole neighbourhood was a vast building site, rapidly morphing into a modern shiny complex. It had always amazed her, how good London was at transforming itself, seamless and silent. Very much unlike Berlin, where they had made a great fuss about Potsdamer Platz, proud of the never-ending building site.

She stopped at the crossroads by King's Cross Station. There was the tree behind the railing where poems and photos had been posted after 7/7. Only a few weeks ago the little square around this tree had been a memorial. She wondered why there was no plaque with the names of the victims, nothing that remembered the events of 7/7. Historical events were shared with more people then ever before, but at the same time they seemed to be forgotten quicker. The tree was lost, fading in its setting. King's Cross had moved on, a new act had begun and the tree had become irrelevant; like an old useless prop that had been overlooked and left on stage by mistake.

A young couple were kissing just in front of the railings, on the same spot where she and Anthony had joined the queue to lay down flowers. What had happened on this spot a hundred years ago? The whole city was littered with the scars of history. Every now and then the present was colliding with the past, like when they were digging out the tunnel for the high-speed train and stumbled upon old graves and scattered bones.

Claire drove up Pentonville Road, thinking of the layers of forgotten history beneath her, forgotten lives, the remnants of generations past. Every society leaves its mark on the surface of the city, creating a new layer, just like a growth ring. What would they leave? High-speed trains, silently rushing under sea level, sleek designed buildings of glass and new, light materials. And in the midst of this had been those young men walking around in trainers and FitnessFirst rucksacks, fiddling with pay-as-you-go phones, while their young, clueless hearts were brimming with dark, old crusted hatred.

Claire was taken aback when Nora slung her arms around her. She stepped back instinctively, as if showing affection openly in front of her mother was somehow inappropriate. But Mrs Ross smiled. She didn't seem to mind that her daughter liked her.

On this particular day Claire was too absent-minded to notice Nora gliding into the water with no hesitation. Only when she saw her swimming in front of her did she realise that Nora had finally conquered her worst fear. It had happened almost behind her back, by accident, just when she hadn't been expecting it. Claire clapped her hands, told her what a brave girl she was. Nora did it again, swam the whole length of the pool, back and forth. She wanted to please Claire, show her that she was a good girl.

Claire looked at Nora with a sense of achievement; she was kicking her legs confidently, swimming in even strokes without any muddle or panic. Suddenly it looked so easy, but she had only reached this level because Claire hadn't insisted and because they had actually left the pool and done other things. Now the pool was not a vast ocean where she could drown. She knew she could just swim to the ladder and get out. Claire liked to believe she had given her something for life, the realisation that fear didn't necessarily mean the end of something – it could just as well be the starting point.

After the class, Claire handed over the certificate to Mrs Ross with a robotic motion. Her job was done; now she would have to let Nora go.

At first she didn't understand what Mrs Ross was saying. "You know, Nora doesn't warm to people easily." Claire nodded; she realised that. "She likes you a lot. It would be just one day a week." Miss Ross looked at her, waiting for an answer.

Claire tried not to let on how happy she would be to look after Nora. But would Anthony approve of such an arrangement? Probably not. They swapped numbers. Claire promised to give her an answer by the following day. She hopped on her scooter with a sense of relief. Nora hadn't been taken from her; if she wanted to she could see her once a week.

On her way home she took another route, avoiding the passage where she had been blocked. A group of youngsters gathered outside the housing estate facing City Road. Some of them had their hoods pulled over their heads. They were smoking, dealing drugs that Claire suspected might be crack. Just when she drove past, one of them turned his head in her direction and she heard someone shouting, "There's that bitch!"

It hit her like a whiplash. They had noticed her, singled her out. Never before had she been so quick to lock her scooter and disappear into the house. Looking through the spyhole in the door, she told herself not to be so ridiculous, not to feel intimidated by teenagers. In recent weeks more cars had been vandalised. Anthony dismissed it as petty crime, but the area seemed to be deteriorating quickly. When they first moved in she had rarely seen broken glass from smashed car windows on the pavement; now it was a daily sight. Hackney's crime scene seemed to overspill into parts of Islington, slowly swallowing it up street by street. She kept her growing concern to herself, though – it would only frustrate Anthony as they weren't able to move house. Especially now, when they had to save every penny for the impending IVF treatment. For the foreseeable future, holidays and meals in restaurants were a luxury they would have to do without.

When Anthony came home that evening he was walking on air. Despite the recent mistake, he had been invited on a weekend golf trip to Scotland with senior work colleagues – a sign he was still in the race for a promotion. The Scotland trip was good news, although she couldn't quite understand what the point was of these 'away trips'. "It's all about bonding and team spirit," Anthony explained. Probably a lot of drinking and cracking sleazy jokes too, she reckoned.

It was just after supper when Dave popped by to watch the Arsenal game with Anthony. But the game was incidental; he clearly wanted to talk with him. Claire could tell from that intense, restless look in his eyes that something troubled him. She went upstairs, immersing herself in a hot bath, leaving the door open so she could eavesdrop. It was too tempting listening to boys' talk.

Dave hadn't been invited to Scotland. Claire wasn't surprised; after all he wasn't the kind of guy who would get a promotion. He hated the City more than anything, the phoniness, the power games, the greed. He wasn't comfortable with the survival-of-the-fittest principle that ruled, the kill-or-get-eaten attitude. Essentially he wasn't a meat-eater, but a fair-haired vegetarian who was exposed to a world of predators. She pricked her ears as he told Anthony how worried he was about losing his job.

"I'm telling you, there will be a reshuffle at the company soon, a big clear out. And I'll be the first to go. I know it and I'm preparing myself."

"Man, you are paranoid," she heard Anthony reply. "How do you know all this shit, anyway?"

"I heard some senior guys talking over lunch... they were serious. The gravy train of economic growth is over. The seven meagre years follow the seven fat years. That's the way it goes. I'm just saving up some money while I can. We are working in a fucking house of cards on the brink of collapse."

"Don't talk like that; I hate this defeatist attitude of yours!" Anthony responded, angrily. "You are worried about losing your job just because you overheard a conversation at lunch? You probably got the wrong end of the stick. Get some perspective." Usually Anthony was mad with Dave when he knew his friend had a point. Claire had always been fascinated by the way they could be rude to each other, even call each other names and still stay friends. By now she leaning over the rim of the bathtub, all ears.

"I've got perspective, believe me," Dave returned. "More than that, I actually I see the bigger picture. I know what's important and what's not and this job is not important."

"So why don't you just go to fucking California and play 'English Dave' with the babes then?"

"That's exactly what I'm going to do, mate, and I'll send you a postcard. I don't want to sit in your hot seat, not for all the money in the world, and just don't for a second think I'm jealous of your bloody trip to Scotland – playing golf with the big boys. Phew... How pathetic is that!" Dave laughed out loud.

"Of course it is. Of course," Anthony agreed in a bored voice that indicated the conversation was over. The steam was out. Like two rutting stags who'd enough of fighting. More beer cans were opened, someone increased the volume of the telly. Claire couldn't understand what they were talking about now – for the rest of the evening they would probably be like an old couple, in mutual agreement, focusing their attention on the football.

She wasn't sure what to make of their conversation; maybe it was time for Dave to move on and do something else. She wished he had talked to her; she knew what it was like to start a new life in a different place. She almost envied him for having that option, and from the conversation it was clear how different his situation was to that of Anthony, who had a house, a mortgage, her, and maybe soon a baby on the way.

Despite their differences, Dave was Anthony's closest friend. Anthony admired Dave's *laissez-faire* attitude to work and life, something Claire found likeable but not exactly manly. She was naturally attracted to ambition and she wasn't surprised Anthony didn't mention their IVF plans. Even close friends keep secrets from each other. How little one knows. She realised one never gets the full picture of a person, only fragments, little insights, small concessions maybe. Even in their marriage there were unspoken words, secrets to be kept and guarded.

It occurred to her that Anthony would almost certainly be a different person when he was in Scotland with his workmates, living out a side she maybe didn't even know existed. Just as he had once told her that her voice had a different sound when she talked to Anne.

Apparently she changed it according to who she was talking to without even noticing it. She too was made of facets and wasn't even fully aware of it. If she didn't know herself entirely, how much did she know Anthony? He was her husband, she slept next to him every night, breathing the same air; she could rest her head on his chest and listen to his heartbeat; she could take his cock into her as deep as she possibly could and, yet, did she really know what was going on with him?

"You remain a mystery," Anthony had said shortly before their wedding day. Maybe that's as close as it gets, accepting that one never fully understands the other person and 'sharing everything' is an illusion. Everything? In that moment she decided not to let Anthony know about Miss Ross's offer. It would be her little secret. As he would almost certainly be against it, why not avoid the stress by just not telling him.

Claire leaned back in the bathtub, relaxing her shoulders. She looked at her kneecap emerging from the foam, a little white island. At times she could still feel a dull pain, especially when the weather changed. She rubbed her knee. There was a long scar from the kneecap all the way down to the middle of her shin. The scar would never fully disappear. A constant reminder of that doomed day which had changed her life forever. Whenever she tried to remember how it all happened, she could follow her memory only to a certain point and then it broke up abruptly, a mental blank.

What she would never forget was how happy she was that day, walking down Neal Street, humming the tune of her favourite song, *A Perfect Day* by Lou Reed. As usual after her new training, she was almost euphoric; her cheeks still blushing from the exercise, she felt light-headed as the endorphins flowed through her veins. She was more than happy with how things had turned out. Only a few weeks before, she had been chosen to dance for the company, and it was as if she was at last doing what she was supposed to.

The first six months after her arrival in London she had been throwing herself into taking classes and going to auditions and finally she had pulled it off, convincing a choreographer that she could do more than classical ballet. All those years of ballet had given her a sound foundation on which she could build and break away from at the same time. Gradually she stepped out of the corset of strict rules, dancing outside the box of tradition, embracing new steps and movements. The choreographer, a Nigerian who had grown up in London, praised her technique and, even more, her passion. "The bit you can't learn," as he put it – words that resonated with her. His dance company was young and increasingly popular, with sold-out performances all over London. It was a colourful mix of people, all from different backgrounds, some older then her. Immediately she felt at ease with them; they asked her about life in Berlin, a city everyone seemed fascinated by. For them, she was exotic, the lanky Swedish girl with the German accent and the impeccable technique who had to learn to loosen up a bit.

On that fateful summer day, as she walked down Neal Street, the sky had cleared from the morning thunder and changed into a polished blue, she felt a rare and deep sense of contentment. Everything had fallen into place. All her fears and doubts had resolved, and not for a second did she regret her move. Whenever she reported back to Anne and her parents she couldn't help but enthuse about it all.

"You sound like Sinbad the sailor, who has found the way to open the door to the treasure," Anne joked on the phone when she'd told her about the successful audition.

"That's exactly what it feels like," Claire had responded.

Although she lived in a much smaller flat than in Berlin, in a constantly littered, run-down street in Holloway, she felt liberated as if a huge space had been opened before her. Sitting on top of a bus she realised how much at home she felt. It was packed full and she could make out about four different languages at one time. Everyone on the bus was a stranger, just like her. As she listened to this babel of voices, permeated with foreign sounds, she was in the cocoon of this bus, thrown together with all these people driving in the same direction, and she felt at home. All on her own and yet mysteriously connected to everyone around her, a rush of happiness flowing through her, almost lifting her out of her seat.

She felt in love without knowing with what or whom; just to be one of the people on this bus was enough to set her alight, and she realised that this was only possible because she had taken a risk; it would never have happened if she had stayed in Berlin, and the complete freedom she experienced in that very moment was exactly the way she wanted to live and dance.

Helena, her Swedish flatmate, was in her second year at RADA. They shared two tiny rooms, a shower and a kitchenette. "In London people live like rats," Helena said, but she said it matter-of-factly, as if she didn't care. She too was in love with the city and she would have put up with anything just to be there.

Claire liked her at once. Helena was just as devoted to her acting as Claire was to dancing. Her passion for acting was profound and she certainly didn't waste her time. Every free minute she rushed off to see a play somewhere. Claire liked to watch her when she was learning a new role, and Helena liked being watched.

"Take me under you microscope," Helena said, learning her first Shakespeare role, and there in the kitchenette she immersed herself in her character, playing it all out. Claire looked at her in awe as she

into Ophelia. The role suited her northern
although her waif-like appearance became
. and more dishevelled as she started to lose
.eight, living on lingonberry jam and krisprolls. After
two weeks she looked perfectly suicidal. Sometimes
Claire wasn't sure whether Helena was in character or
herself anymore. She heard her moaning in the
shower, talking to Hamlet and ghosts. Her eyes got
bigger as if they had seen too much, widened to the
verge of insanity.

One night, Helena crept into Claire's bed. "I am so
glad not to be alone," she said, squeezing her hand.
"Soon I will be dead and buried."

Claire was surprised how tiny her hand felt, like the
hand of a scared child. She looked at her from the side,
at her delicate profile that seemed even more fragile,
porcelain-like in the dark, and it was as if Helena was
just a reflection of herself. There they were lying in
bed, in a city of eight million people and eight million
dreams, holding on to each other, stranded by the tide
of the night.

Listening to the noises, relentlessly permeating their
bedroom, emergency sirens, the drunken shouting of
late pub-goers and the permanent murmur of traffic,
Claire couldn't sleep. She was thinking of all the new
steps she had learnt, like the words of a new language
that put together in the right order finally made sense.
She had the urge to get up and dance in the dark of the

room, her heart beating fast with excitement, synchronised to the rhythm of the city that was forever moving, self-engrossed in its own eternal dance, never coming to a halt.

When Claire thought back to those early days in London it was with a sense of nostalgic sentiment and gratitude. After all, it was because of Helena that she had met Anthony. Helena had literally dragged her out that evening, waving film tickets at her while she was doing yoga on the living room floor. Claire left the house only reluctantly. And it was there in the dark of the cinema that they realised that their seats were double booked. There were two young men already sitting there. Claire remembered them wearing suits, as if they had just come from work, somehow looking smug, giving off an über-confident, annoying vibe.

They were comparing the tickets that had the same seat numbers but, "Sorry girls," was all they could come up with. As all the seats were occupied, all they could do was get their money back and leave. Helena was furious. "City boys," she said dismissively, storming out the cinema. "They could have offered us their seats!"

Thinking back to how Anthony and Dave were sitting there, holding on to their tickets resolutely, made her laugh. Never in a million years would she have thought to hook up with one of them.

However, a week later at a Wagamama restaurant in Islington, as she was eating her favourite noodle soup, someone tapped her on the shoulder. "I know your friend was really mad at us but frankly, you didn't miss anything. The film was rubbish."

She recognised him immediately. The bottle-green eyes and dark hair. Anthony. She liked his name. He sat next to her and two hours later they were still there, talking. He insisted on inviting her and Helena to a film, to make up for their ruined evening.

She didn't fall in love with a bang. It was a smooth transition, a gradual development. The sex was relaxed and grown up, no fumbling and gawky gestures. No blush with shame. He was a good cook too, which Claire was convinced came with being a good lover. Maybe she fell in love as she watched him filetting that turbot, his hands disappearing in the cavity of the fish, stuffing it with lemon and herbs. He was different, not the dark arty type she usually went for.

"As soon as he finds out what a neurotic mess I am, it's over," Claire told Helena as if to protect herself. But he seemed to even out her mood swings, shrugging them off with a generosity she had never experienced before. As a result, she became calmer; she wasn't walking on quicksand anymore, but on solid ground. Although she didn't quite know where it was going, she knew early on that with Anthony she was in for the long run.

What was so maddening in hindsight was that she didn't really have to cross that street. Just because she decided at the last minute to get something from a shop before heading home, she suddenly changed direction. She couldn't even remember what it was she wanted from that shop. The car hit her just as she stepped off the pavement. Screeching tyres, a loud bang, and being lifted off the floor is all she could remember before she lost consciousness.

According to the report she flew a few metres across the street, shattering her leg with full force on the kerb of the pavement. The driver, a woman who had just been given a silver Honda Civic for her 18th birthday, had immediately called an ambulance. Not used to left-hand traffic, Claire had simply looked in the wrong direction.

She knew something was wrong with her left leg the moment she opened her eyes. She couldn't feel nor move it. It was there, propped up and covered in a white cast. A drip was hanging next to her bed, connected to a vein in her hand through a curly plastic tube. She could see bruises on her arm; she was probably bruised all over her body. She felt battered as if she had suffered a prolonged beating, but she couldn't feel any pain.

"You are on a high dose of morphine," the orthopaedic surgeon said. He was young and he smiled as he leaned over her, testing her temperature on her forehead with his hand. "You are doing very well, darling." First she looked at him and then at her leg. There was only one thing she wanted to know.

He sighed, pushed the chair next to her as close as possible. "Claire," he said, patting her hand apologetically. His voice was soft and smooth. "I know this is going to be hard for you. Your knee has a complicated fracture; you won't be able to dance again, but you are lucky that you will be able to walk."

Everything was white, the walls, the curtains, the cast, the doctor's coat, even his teeth seemed to oscillate. The numbness followed almost immediately after he left the room. It was as if the cast wasn't only on her leg but now all around her, inside her, keeping everything tight and together, completely motionless. Even her thoughts seemed to be stored as if in the little compartments of an ice cube tray, clear and frozen. Staring into the air she was waiting for tears to fill her eyes, blurring her vision, taking away the edge, but her eyes stayed dry. Maybe that was the worst, this inability to cry. Instead, a strange, deadly stillness wrapped her up like the bandages of a mummy.

The door opened; Helena was the first to visit, then came her mates from the dance company. They brought flowers, books, chocolates. She heard herself saying "thank you," but it sounded hollow, like an echo from someone else who was miles away. She knew there and then that she would never see any of her dance colleagues again; the word 'dancing' wasn't in her vocabularly anymore, eradicated forever.

Anthony came to visit; it was hard to look into his eyes. "You don't have to come," she said. But he visited, every day. Something she could look forward to in the daily routine of dreary meals and doctors' visits. When he couldn't visit because he was doing overtime at work he would send flowers. Yellow lilies, roses, a white orchid, its delicate paper-thin blossom trembling with every draft in the air. She looked at those flowers, as if they were a part of Anthony and something deep inside her shifted, a sheer unbearable longing to let go and cry inconsolably into his dark hair. But when he came, sitting next to her at the bed, holding her hand, her voice was dry and sober and completely detached as if it were a creature on its own that had nothing to do with her.

Her parents called. Mother started to sob almost immediately and Claire ended up comforting her, which was somehow much easier to bear than being pitied. "I'll be alright. I'm lucky to be alive!"

That was the sentence she repeated again and again, although she didn't mean it; it was like pushing a button – an entirely mechanical act. Her parents wanted to visit her immediately, but she made them promise her not to. Under no circumstances did she want them or Anne to see her in that misery. The sheer thought of them, surrounding the bed, their eyes fixated on her leg, stretched out like an exclamation mark, made her shiver. It would have been unbearably degrading. Instead, Anne and her parents organised a counsellor.

"A shrink?" Claire asked, almost amused.

"We think it could help you," her mother said in a concerned voice. "If you can't see your own family. You need someone to talk to."

"Alright then," Claire agreed, just so her mother wouldn't start crying again, sobbing into the receiver. It felt like a deal, that maybe they needed to do that for her, so they could feel they were Doing Something.

The psychotherapist came, asking her how she felt. She could see a tunnel at the exit of the hospital that she would have to walk through when she was released, a dark narrow tunnel with no end in sight. But she didn't say that; she said, "Nothing. I feel nothing." He nodded, writing something in his notebook before he started talking about "drawing up a map for the future." The word hurt. Future. She told him to fuck off. He closed the door behind him carefully as if she was asleep. But he came back, week after week – she almost admired his persistence.

"You are not going to fix my leg, are you? So why are you wasting my time?"

"I'm trying to talk about your feelings, Claire. Maybe I can help you to get over it."

"Over it? Over what? There is nothing to get over. Apparently I'm lucky."

"You are, you just can't feel it at the moment."

"You're damn right."

"Are you angry?"

She didn't answer. What was he doing here, apart from getting on her nerves? He prescribed pills. "Your brain is much too low on serotonin," he explained. "This will lighten up your mood a bit," he said with a knowing smile. "You will soon feel much better."

Reading the leaflet of the medication, Claire was surprised to learn that the pills weren't just some mild mood enhancer, but to treat clinical depression.

A few days later she could think clearly again, although she didn't feel much better. But at least she had a plan.

"I'm not what I used to be. When I'm out of here, I will be a different person," she explained to Anthony. "I am thinking of going back to Berlin. Living with my parents for a while and sorting things out."

"I'm afraid that's not going to happen," he replied, walking up and down the room as if he had to measure its size. It was his self-confidence and his certainty that blew her away. He didn't actually ask her to marry him, he ordered her to it. Like some medicine that had to be forced down her throat. "Just so you know what's going to happen when you're out of here."

As soon as he had left, she asked the nurse for a mirror. Never before had she felt so unattractive, propped up in bed, toad-like with greasy hair and pimply skin.

She couldn't help but smile for the first time since the accident. Surely this was the time she was at her weakest and lowest, and she couldn't have been more unprepared and surprised as she lay there in the hospital bed, feeling useless and damaged on every level, someone was willing to take her hand and lead her life in a completely different direction yet again. Maybe it is a good thing, she told herself, that the worst must have happened already.

*

She saw them coming out of the house. Mother and daugther. Mrs Ross had her arm on Nora's shoulder, guiding and protecting her at the same time. Seeing them together like that, an unbreakable pair, gave Claire a pang and she realised how alike they looked. Both had delicate features, lean elegant bodies and fair skin. No doubt Nora would one day turn into a beauty just like her mother, and she wondered what it felt like to have a miniature version of oneself. What did Mrs Ross feel when she looked at her daughter? So many things would remain a mystery to Claire as long as she didn't have her own child, so many questions would stay unanswered. However, the attachment she felt for Nora was real and painful, and she couldn't help but feel a rush of happiness when she ran towards her, arms stretched out.

Claire held her up, laughing; she could feel her warm cheek on her face. It was their first day out. Mrs Ross had already retreated into the car, waved goodbye to them with a quick half-smile, and driven off. Claire envied her coolness, her relaxed state of mind. She didn't have to earn Nora's love; she was her mother and would always have the advantage. Even if she neglected her daughter she still would be loved by her. The bond created through genes and blood was inevitably stronger than anything she could ever offer. Claire hailed a cab. Nora loved riding through the city in a black cab and Claire loved treating her like a little princess.

There she was, sitting on the edge of the seat, lollipop in mouth. "Are we going right up there?" Nora asked excitedly, pointing at the white wheel of the London Eye as the taxi crossed Southwark Bridge. The sky was clear; they would have a good view. It was something Claire had wanted to do for a long time, to get a bird's eye view of London and capture its vastness.

The capsule-shaped cabin was bigger then she'd expected. Slowly they were lifted into the air; they could see the bend of the Thames and the grand line-up of Westminster, Big Ben and the white dome of St. Paul's Cathedral. Soon they were over the rooftops and buildings became smaller, like randomly assorted toys lining the streets, which meandered in every direction. They looked like the tentacles of an ever-growing beast insatiably feeding on the land that surrounded it.

On the right, the skyscrapers of Canary Wharf were stubbornly poking into the sky. Somewhere in that urban jungle of glass and steel was Anthony, sitting at a computer in a sleek open-plan office, analysing numbers and making economic predictions. Claire remembered what Dave had said about the house of cards that was about to collapse. From this height, the giant company logos looked tiny and somehow unreal. London was gradually sinking back, appearing vulnerable and fragile under the huge sky, now almost uncannily changing to a different shade. Nora meanwhile was all upbeat, pressing her nose against the window and chatting to another girl. Claire could see that the girl's mother was younger than her, probably in her mid-twenties.

"How old is yours?" the woman suddenly asked her. She had just assumed Nora was her child, and why not? They even had the same blonde hair.

"Seven," Claire answered without hesitation.

"Same age as mine then," the woman said with a contented smile. But Claire immediately regretted that she had let this woman believe she was Nora's mother. It was as if she had opened a floodgate, and the woman wouldn't stop asking all sorts of questions about the school Nora went to and whether she plans to have a sibling for her.

"Actually, I am three months pregnant," Claire said in

the hope this would shut her up, but it just got worse. The broodiness was almost palpable and the cabin became increasingly claustrophobic. Stuck with this woman who observed her closely, eyeing up her belly as if looking for the evidence, she couldn't wait to get out. However, the wheel of the London Eye turned agonisingly slowly. At the top they seemed to stop for minutes, with the city spread out down below. A sudden attack of vertigo forced Claire to sit down.

"Are you alright?" the woman asked. "Maybe you shouldn't have come up here, being pregnant."

Nora suddenly turned her head. "Are you going to have a baby?" she asked bluntly.

The situation couldn't have been more awkward. What could she do other than continue the lie unless she wanted to appear a complete fool? She had no choice. "Yes, my darling," she said, stroking the crown of her head, "but the baby won't be here for a long time."

The woman looked at her, with a puzzled expression, probably wondering how Nora didn't know already that she would be getting a sibling. As if she realised she had stepped too far into a stranger's private territory, or through uncertainty, she retreated to the other end of the cabin to tend to her daughter.

Claire heaved a sigh of relief. How could she have put herself in a situation like this? So as not to raise further suspicion and to make sure the woman wouldn't speak to her again, she talked to Nora about other trips around London they could do, like going to the zoo and the aquarium, where they could see tropical fish from all over the world. But the more she talked about it, the more miserable she felt. It was inevitable there would be situations like this again, that she would be mistaken for Nora's mother and, flattering though it was, it was also deeply hurtful. But to admit she was just the babysitter would be worse.

There was no way to end the dilemma but to stop seeing Nora for good, to take herself out of this painful situation. She had too much at stake. How foolish of her to ever think this arrangement would work out. She now blamed herself, biting her lips. An awkward silence had filled the cabin, even the girls had stopped talking to each other, and Claire counted the seconds until they reached the bottom.

"Good luck," the woman said as the cabin finally came to a halt and the door opened, but Claire couldn't look at her. She just rushed off, her head between her shoulders – it was as if she had scam written all over her.

Walking along the promenade by the Thames, watching the boats pass by, Claire had to fight back the tears. She wouldn't tell Nora; she just wanted to make the most of this last day with her, to cherish and enjoy every minute they had left. At an ice-cream stand she bought her a chocolate ice-cream. Nora was humming a tune while she licked at the cone. With one hand holding the ice cream, and the other gently touching the railing as she strolled past, she seemed completely absorbed in her own little world. How wonderful it must be to be able to daydream like a child, to live in the moment like that, unbothered by the future and past. And as she watched Nora enjoying her ice cream, it was as if she were eating it herself. She could almost taste the cold creamy sweetness of the chocolate on her tongue.

Maybe that is one of the reasons people have children, so they can go through all the stages of childhood again, with all its monstrosities, joys and thousand little miracles. She wondered whether Nora would one day, when she was a young woman, remember the lightness of this moment, remember the scent of the summer air, slightly cooler near the river. Or maybe she would just forget her as soon as she was out of sight, and what was such a precious moment for Claire was just a pleasant but forgettable interlude in this young child's life.

'Surgical cut' were the two words in her mind when she phoned Mrs Ross. The conversation was surprisingly short. She had planned to tell her about new work commitments, but Mrs Ross wasn't interested in an explanation. Her voice was friendly and distant as usual. She understood immediately, thanked her for everything and hung up. From now on she would have to focus on pursuing their own dream, their own family.

It was bad luck that it was the day Anthony had left

for Scotland. Without him the house felt bigger. Her footsteps resonated. Claire roamed the rooms as if she was looking for him. Everywhere she stumbled over traces he had left behind, a sock on the floor, his dressing gown lying inside out on the bed. In the garden she found the tongs they had forgotten about from the barbecue, the tips black from the burnt coal.

Subdued voices came from the neighbours' house. She wished the boys would come out and play football again, kick the ball against the brick wall, so she could hear the squeaking sound of their trainers; she missed their shouting and laughter, the comforting sound of children playing. She noticed that most of the plants she had bought were already dead, some covered in tiny fat greenflies, others eaten away by snails and slugs, the ground covered with their white slimy trail. They were now hidden somewhere but soon they would come out again to continue their attack. The rose and passionflower had become completely interwoven, as if they were fighting for space on the wall, suffocating each other.

She was taken aback by the cruel ugliness of the flowerbed. It was frustrating to think that only a few weeks ago she had spent a whole day on it, trying to make it look nice. She could have wrestled with weeds, digging up the dry soil, irrigating the hard crumbly earth, but the prospect of going into the empty house when dusk was falling was somehow just unbearable. Being on her own seemed like walking into the dark throat of a predator from which she could never come out again. For a moment she just stood there, unable to move, paralysed by an overwhelming sense of being lost. She felt like a beetle that senses danger and just freezes on the spot, pretending to be dead already.

It was the thought of Sadie that released her from her apathy. She was the only person she knew she could go to. She didn't even bother to put some makeup on; she just rushed out of the house, leaving the lights on so that when she came back it would look like someone was already there.

In a cobbled passage in Covent Garden, she heard the rasping smoky voice of Nina Simone from afar. Sadie had turned the music on high volume, leaving the door of the shop open. She threw herself towards her and Sadie pressed her against her breast. "Darling," Sadie said, frowning, "look at you. All worn out! I am going to cook you dinner. I have just one more customer to serve. Go and find yourself something nice to wear," and she pushed her towards a rail of dresses.

The shop was a treasure trove and the clothes had the light, musky scent of amber, as if Sadie had worn them all, putting her stamp on them. Every dress bore the promise of a different life. Sadie had lived through them all and was now ready to give them up for others to experience. Here in Sadie's little kingdom she felt protected and safe. And she was grateful that she didn't have to ask, Sadie realised immediately that Claire couldn't be on her own tonight. Browsing through a rail of dresses she heaved a sigh of relief when she heard her on the phone cancelling a date with Paolo. Suddenly she heard a familiar voice. Turning, she saw Mrs Ross stride out of the changing room and plant herself in front of the mirror. She was wearing a cobalt blue floor-length gown with batwing sleeves.

Claire hid behind the dresses, her mouth open, as Sadie shouted, "What do you think, Claire?" When she emerged from behind the rail, their eyes met immediately. "May I introduce you to my friend Deborah, the wonderful actress," Sadie said, obviously proud of her glamorous friend.

"We know each other," Mrs Ross said, somewhat startled to see her there. "She taught my daughter to swim. And she just quit her job as her nanny." She smiled and added, "Never mind, Nora almost liked you too much!"

Claire nodded but didn't say anything; she was much too baffled by the situation and too busy working out the relationship Mrs Ross had with Sadie. She remembered the dragonfly necklace she had seen in Mrs Ross's house and now it was clear. It must have come from Sadie, a gift.

Claire could instantly tell that Sadie adored Mrs Ross, and possibly even had a crush on her. "Turn around," she said, moving her hands as if conducting an orchestra.

The light cobalt blue fabric was flowing around her tall, slender body. "You are a goddess!" Sadie shrieked, unable to take her eyes off her.

Maybe it was a pang of jealously that grasped Claire, almost taking her breath away for a moment. Wasn't it enough that she was Nora's mother; did she have to be so beautiful as to take all of Sadie's attention too?

Mrs Ross bought the dress, promising Sadie to give her tickets to the premiere of her next play, in which she was playing the lead. "Maybe you could come too," she said generously to Claire, and then she left, leaving behind a whiff of her expensive perfume.

"She's just one of those women..." Sadie said, sighing, "strong, independent, everyone at her feet, yet incredibly lonely. No man would ever get or understand her, or be able to make her happy."

"So you are the one, then?" Claire said, laughing aloud. "Deborah Ross's saviour."

"I can tell she is not averse."

"To what?"

"To lesbianism."

For a moment she contemplated the concept of Mrs Ross and Sadie as a couple – it was hysterical, but then, why not?

"Well," Claire said, "I wish you the best of luck and, if it ever comes to you running off with Mrs Deborah Ross, I would be happy to play the role of Nora's mother."

That evening in Sadie's kitchen, over one of her culinary concoctions, Claire told her about their plan to try IVF, the anxiety and the heartache, and she told her about Nora, even how she trespassed into Mrs Ross's house, and her decision to stop seeing Nora for good. It was just after midnight when Sadie got up, carrying the empty wine glasses to the sink.

"I just never had that. That urge for a child; it just wouldn't work for me at all. It remains a mystery to me why any woman would want to burden herself with so much responsibility," Sadie confessed. "I look after my friends; I look after you," she said. "That's enough for me."

"You are looking after me alright," Claire said, taking her hand in a sudden urge to be physically close. She regretted it immediately; she didn't want Sadie to think she would play around with her or was sexually interested. As if she had read her thoughts, Sadie laughed out loud. "Don't be so paranoid," she chuckled, "you can take my hand and I won't rape you."

Claire looked down, embarassed. "I'd better go now," she muttered, trying to get up, dizzy from all the wine.

"You are not going anywhere," Sadie insisted, shepherding her into her bedroom. It had the same familiar scent of amber, something oriental and sensuous. Warm from the wine and enveloped in Sadie's smell she gave in, undressed to her underwear and slipped into the cool satin sheets of her bed.

She looked as Sadie was undressing herself in the half-lit room. "I hope you don't mind; I always sleep naked." But it wasn't awkward to have Sadie naked next to her, and she didn't mind as Sadie tenderly stroked her back. Claire relaxed, feeling like a cat in its basket, all curled up, warm and cosy.

"Sleep well," Sadie murmured, kissing her on the forehead. Closing her eyes and, slowly drifting off, she thought of Helena, who was far away, trying her luck in LA. She hoped she was alright and not getting beaten up by life too much. Maybe that was what it all came down to, surviving, and being content with the simple fact that one was lucky to be still alive.

Anthony couldn't hide his disappointment when he called on the way home. The trip to Scotland hadn't had the bonding effect with his colleagues he had expected. Although he was now on another level and would soon be promoted, he suddenly seemed uneasy with his newly-acquired position. Never before had he questioned the way the bank did business, but he was now talking of amoral practices and irresponsible risks. Maybe Dave's words have finally got through to him.

"I know this comes at the worst time, but I don't know how much longer I can do this job." It was as much a confession as a warning, but Claire wasn't concerned yet; maybe he was just nervous because of his new responsibilities.

He would have to get used to it. That's at least what she told Anne on the phone as she was cooking Anthony's favourite meal to welcome him back home. She was talking to her sister while basting the roast chicken. Anne had sent her a picture of Margarethe on her BlackBerry, looking round and happy, a tattered Paddington Bear under her arm. His left eye was missing; Maragrethe had plucked it out, fascinated by the round cold glass. Anne and Claire were laughing about the complete ignorance babies have about things, destroying everything they could get their hands on, when she suddenly heard a loud rumbling noise coming from the hallway upstairs.

Immediately she went to put the phone down. "What is it?" she heard her sister shout from the other end. But Claire didn't answer. There was Anthony standing by the door, blood all over his face.

"Quick!" he said in a shaky voice, grabbing the phone. While he called the police, Claire stepped outside and looked down the half-lit street. But there was no one there. At the end of the street she could see the slow-moving traffic of City Road. Anthony was bleeding from his ear. "There were two of them. I couldn't see properly; it was dark. One had a hammer."

Ten minutes later two young, heavily-built policeman were standing in the living room, one of them taking a swab from Anthony's face with a Q-tip. "Maybe we can match the DNA with an existing offender," he explained. "You will have to come into the station to have a look at our database; you might remember their faces when you see some pictures."

A minute later they were gone. Claire stood in front of the house watching the police car speed away with Anthony sitting in the back. No doubt these were kids from the estate. She noticed he didn't have his bag when he came in – of course they had taken it. He could have been beaten to death for his laptop bag. She went back down into the kitchen and found the roast chicken was black.

Anthony came back from the police station half an hour later. She put some ice on his cheek, which had turned violet. He hadn't been able to indentify his attackers. "You won't believe how big their database is," he said. "They told me violent crime in this area has doubled in the last two years."

"They'll probably never find the bastards," Claire said angrily. "I'm sure that not too far away they're celebrating their successful haul."

Anthony put his hand on her shoulder as if to calm her down. "Somewhere down the line these guys are victims themselves."

She looked at him, amazed that he could be so philosophical about it, as if forgiving them. It was as if he had aged in a very short time. That night, Anthony held on to her like a shipwrecked sailor to a piece of wood.

How easily she could have lost him that night, to a random pointless attack. She listened to his breathing, waiting for it to become deeper, slowly taking on the rhythm of sleep. It was as if the attackers had kicked them out of their own house. Claire was alarmed by every noise. From afar she could hear the helicopter again, but this time it didn't come closer. Finally they had chosen a different spot to observe.

It seemed they had been waiting for something like this to happen. Her parents, Anne and even Karl urged her to move back to Germany. It didn't help that she told them an attack like this could happen in any city in the world. Since the bombings they were convinced London was an extraordinarily dangerous place.

"Just think about if you ever have children. Do you think this is a good place to grow up?" The blame in her mother's voice was impossible to ignore.

Claire took a deep breath and sat down. "Yes, in fact I think London is an excellent place to grow up, because this is a real city with real problems and not a fucking fairytale!" She was surprised by her own anger. The immediate silence that followed was almost loud. "I'm sorry, Mum," she said, in a more measured tone, "but that's the way it is. We are staying in London, no matter what."

Her mother called her stubborn and unreasonable, but Claire didn't mind her criticism anymore. She had her place in the family: she was the difficult one, the one with her own mind. And she knew now that it would always be like that.

****

It was one of those days between seasons, when summer draws to a close and the mornings suddenly become much cooler. They breathed the late September air, fallen leaves, the crisp smell of autumn. Anthony put the collar of his jacket up, wrapping his arm around her to keep her warm. Claire looked at him from the side. Whatever happens they would still have each other. They had discussed it over and over again, and maybe this is was as good as it gets. To have someone you could stick things out with. Since her decision, she felt a huge weight had been lifted from her shoulders. Though it was still very early, the waiting room of the clinic was completely full.

Couples and single women were sitting silently, reading or watching a tennis match on the little TV in the corner. Claire couldn't help but stare at the women, guessing their age, scanning their faces for signs of hope and fear. She overheard a muttered conversation between two of them, comparing the numbers of follicles they had produced. Even here in the waiting room of a fertility clinic there was competiton.

Although she felt calm and together, her palms were

moist when the doctor came in and called their names. It was their initial consultation. The doctor looked like a friendly angel, with her white coat and merciful smile. But the angel didn't beat about the bush; her words were clear. "You have no time to waste. The sooner you start the better." She went on to show them statistics of the clinic's success rates. The graphics on her computer screen were impressive as she talked them through the whole procedure. She spoke about follicles and blasto-cysts, acronyms like IUI and ICSI.

"We offer counselling as well, of course. For some couples this can be the most stressful time in their lives. And I'm afraid you'll have to take at least a month off work," she said, looking at Claire. "This is a full-time commitment. You will have to come in every day for blood tests and scans, up to three times a day and some-times at very short notice."

Claire nodded; it sounded like a hell of a schedule.

"Not exactly the most romantic way to have a baby. Being conceived in a petri dish," Anthony said as they left the clinic, clutching a brochure with a smiling baby on it and a whole folder of consent forms under his arm. "But we knew that, didn't we?" Claire replied calmly.

The sun peeked out from behind the clouds now and then, immersing London in bright light for a few minutes before hiding again. For a moment they just stood there as if they weren't quite sure what to do next. "Let's walk through the park," Anthony suggested and took her hand.

At this time of day, Regent's Park was almost empty. "Look at this," he said, his fingers combing through a stretch of tall silver grass. It was surprisingly soft. She plucked a blade and stroked him, the tender tip of the grass gliding over his skin. She saw the fine hair on his forearm stand up, forming goosebumps, just like the rippling of water when one threw a stone into a still lake.

Suddenly they both looked up as a flock of birds flew overhead, a black compact cloud. There was no lead bird; the group flew as a single unit. As if following the lead of an invisible conductor, they formed synchronised shapes in the sky. A perfectly coordinated aerial dance. Then, as if by mutual agreement, they changed direction.

Book Group Questions

At Legend Press, we only publish books that are well worth talking about, that will generate conversation, as well as being written by some of the world's top writers and being fantastic reads. After all, the reactions and conversations they generate are what makes books so unique, thought-provoking and so amazing.

A vital part of book conversations are book groups and to be of assistance we've listed a few questions in no particular order that may be worth considering. Whether you take them into account or not, we expect this book to generate debate and please feel free to send us any comments:

info@legend-paperbooks.co.uk

1. How do feel towards the central character, Claire, through and at the end of the novel?

2. Claire and her group of friends are a rangle of mid-thirties character without children. What was your reaction towards them and their depiction?

3. At the time of writing, IVF is a hot topic and is accepted to greatly varying lengths in different countries. How do you feel towards the issue following *The Sky is Changing*?

4. *The Sky is Changing* also reflects on nationality and identity – do you feel this led more to a sense of freedom for isolation in the characters?

5. What are your thoughts on the relationship between Claire and Nora, and Nora's mother, Mrs Ross?

6. How do you feel towards Claire and Anthony's relationship and their desire and efforts to have children?

7. Do you have any thoughts on the structure, pace and style of the narrative? What effect did it have on you, the reader?

8. The book is set within large cities and includes the fall-out and reaction to terrorist attack. Did you have any thoughts on the setting?

9. *The Sky is Changing* touches on increased tension and inner-city intimidation. What effect do you believe this has on Claire and Anthony by the end of the novel?

10. The novel is the first in English by Zoë Jenny – author of the all-time highest-selling debut novel by a Swiss author. What are your overall thoughts on *The Sky is Changing*?

I hope you enjoyed this fantastic novel. Please come and visit us to see Zoë Jenny's work and also other amazing books at Legend Press:

www.legendpress.co.uk